THE SECRET OF SOOTY WICK INN

Elizabeth Lindgren

the Secret of Sooty Wick Inn

Elizabeth Lindgren

Haley's
Athol, Massachusetts

🦌 a Sooty Wick imprint

Haley's
488 South Main Street
Athol, MA 01331
haley.antique@verizon.net
800.215.8805

Copy edited by Lauren Thomas.

Lindgren, Elizabeth.
        The secret of Sooty Wick Inn / Elizabeth Lindgren ; illustrations, Elizabeth Lindgren
    Athol, Mass. : Haley's, 2017.

    160 pages 14.81x21.01cm

SUMMARY: Beetle's parents send her to spend a week in Maine far from her posh home in Back Bay, Boston. Reluctantly, Beetle finds herself in the care of Murtha Bellwether, a mysterious innkeeper. Is Beetle threatened by a dragon moments after her arrival at Murtha's ramshackle inn? Why must she share a bedroom with a devilish cat? Shortly after hunters arrive for their annual stay, Beetle makes a startling discovery. She takes it upon herself to find out Murtha's secret before it's too late only to have the world as she knows it turned upside down.

    1.   Magic — Juvenile fiction. 2. Deer — Juvenile fiction. I. Lindgren, Elizabeth. II. Title.
    ISBN: 978-0-9967730-1-0
    PZ7.1.L554 Se 2016

For Kiley and Reece

Contents

Illustrations

The Reception

The old, ramshackle inn looked even scarier than the boarded-up coffin factory Beetle had seen on the way into town. The thought of having to spend an entire week in the dreadful house made her stomach churn. She wanted to call her parents and have them arrange for her immediate return to her home in Back Bay, Boston. But they had arrived deep in the Peruvian rain forest by now.

Not that it mattered. Beetle sighed. There was no one home. Not even her family's crabby housekeeper, Lydia Blister. She'd left for her annual housekeeping convention in Chicago right after a limousine arrived for Beetle that morning.

Beetle's mom and Murtha Bellwether, the owner of the inn, were old friends. But their friendship did nothing to dispel her unease about staying with the stranger. Beetle was shy by nature, and this was the first time she had been on her own.

Towering spruce trees stood like giant beanstalks behind the inn, casting long menacing shadows across its mossy roof. Brambles, dense as coiled barbed wire, had overrun the yard. To the far right, a row of ancient maples with gnarled trunks and limbs resembled alien life forms.

Averting her troubled gaze, Beetle noticed a weathered gray sign half buried in the ground. Squinting hard at the faint lettering, she just about read *SOOTY WICK INN, Estab. 1720.* She pressed the toe of her ankle boot against one side of the sign and tried to lever it out of the ground. When it didn't budge, she applied more pressure. It resisted for an instant then erupted from its shallow grave and broke apart, raising a damp, moldy stink. A network of pale fungal threads clung to the underside of its rotten boards.

Beetle hadn't meant to break the sign. She had only wanted to get a sense of how long it had lain there. Crouching, she hastily reassembled the jagged pieces as best she could. It wasn't the first time one of her spontaneous investigations resulted in unintended consequences. Regrettably, she had a history of being too curious for her own good. She made a mental note to curb her impulsiveness.

She stood and gazed up at the glowering house. The windows' small multiple panes shone dark and impenetrable, like one-way mirrors. She felt her face flame hot. For all she knew, Murtha could be staring at her right now, thinking she was the sort of girl who had no regard for other people's property.

She tried to visualize what Murtha might look like. In her mind's eye, she shuffled and combined different faces and body types. It was a complete surprise when her imaginings took an unexpected turn, conjuring a dark, cobwebby attic thick with the toxic scent of mothballs and an old trunk with things best forgotten buried deep inside. The image filled her with foreboding.

Was it an omen or a reflection of her sullen mood? She'd had her heart set on spending Thanksgiving recess with her best friend, Stella Piccolo. The recess had been extended from two days to a week because of renovations to the dormitories at the Brattle Academy for Girls that Beetle and Stella attended. Beetle's mom had spoiled her plan the previous night when she informed Beetle she was being sent to the inn instead. When Beetle protested, her mom assured her that she would get along fine with Murtha. In the end, Beetle accepted that she had to go; however, she resolved not to like Murtha as a matter of principle.

She knew it was wrong to take her frustration out on Murtha, but she couldn't help feeling resentful. She shifted her gaze to the house again. The tightly shuttered front door looked as if it hadn't been used in a hundred years. Worms and rot had ravaged most of the front entryway, but enough of it remained to suggest the inn had once been a showplace.

Beetle looked up the gravel driveway and spotted a door in the ell attached to the main house. It was about three in the afternoon, close to the time of her appointed arrival. She braced herself, assuming Murtha would come out the door at any moment. Long minutes passed, however, as Beetle shivered in chill November wind. Loose window shutters banged. Ragged tufts of smoke spewed from a crooked chimney, circling the rooftop like scavenging birds.

Eager to get out of the cold despite her apprehension about meeting Murtha, Beetle finally realized that no one would show up to help her with her heavy suitcase. So she decided to haul it to the side door herself. The small wheels on the bottom were no match for weeds and deep ruts in the driveway.

Beetle guessed the distance to the door was about seventy feet, but the thought of navigating the obstacle course ahead made it seem as long as an airport runway.

Gritting her teeth, she gripped the suitcase's long metal handle with both hands and pulled. The suitcase lurched into motion as Beetle staggered forward. Its small wheels moved sluggishly through rough gravel and tangled weeds. Believing there would be nothing to do at the inn, she'd packed her iPad, cell phone, journal, several boxed paperback sets of Greta Spleen mysteries, and some school books for extra credit assignments, along with her clothes. She hadn't considered the weight of the extra items.

Breathless from her exertion, she paused to rest halfway up the driveway. Her gaze wandered to a moldering jack-o'-lantern slumped on top of a fence post several feet away. Its face was a festering pudding of flesh, the mouth a puckered slash. Only one of its eyes remained open, an empty socket appearing eerily fixated on her. A pea-green Volkswagen bus, long overdue for the scrap heap, stood beside the pumpkin-headed post.

Anxious to leave the grim-looking companions behind, Beetle started across the driveway. An enormous gray barn stood on her left. She hadn't gone far when her suitcase pitched into a rut. After several frustrating attempts, her shoulders aching from the effort, she managed to haul it out. Resentfully, she looked at the inn, wondering why Murtha still hadn't acknowledged her arrival.

Beetle huffed. Did Murtha show the same disregard to all her guests? Perhaps that was the reason the inn had fallen on hard times. The sudden burst of irritation energized her weary limbs. Reaching the cobbled dooryard, at last, she sagged against one of the tall granite posts flanking the entrance.

The inn looked even more depressing up close. Its age-blackened clapboards were cupped and brittle. A spindly rose bush with a single withered bloom clung desperately to a broken trellis next to the side door. Skeletal weeds between the cobbles rattled in the wind like fingers bones on a cannibal's necklace.

An involuntary chill shot up Beetle's spine.

She had barely stepped away from the stone pillar before a wall of wind slammed her from behind. Cocooned in a churning funnel of dirt and dead leaves, she skated across the worn cobbles, suitcase in tow. The wind died suddenly, abandoning her, trembling, at the side door in front of a broad granite step. Spitting out grains of sand and blinking dust from her eyes, she stood on wobbly legs. It took a moment for her to evaluate what had happened. Some kind of freaky whirlwind, she supposed.

Groaning with effort, she wrestled her suitcase onto the step and clambered up after it. A rough-grained wooden door stood within arm's reach. Horizontal rows of rusty, square-headed nails studded the vertical planking. Their reddish-brown coating looked like dried blood. Pushing the sickening thought from her mind, she looked up at the sky and searched for a patch of blue between scudding clouds. A strangled scream stuck in her throat as she beheld a black dragon perched on the peak of the inn's gabled end.

Iridescent as a black pearl, the dragon stood tall like an upended school bus. Tendrils of blue smoke curled from bony nostrils as the beast studied her through cold reptilian eyes, salivating.

Beetle cowered behind her suitcase and whimpered when the dragon raked its long, spiky tail over the inn's roof. She raised her arms to shield her head from shattered wood shingles and bits of

a dragon on the roof

It must be Murtha!

moss raining down. Then the dragon thrust its great beaky head over the side of the building and opened its cruel jaws, baring several rows of long serrated teeth.

Shaking uncontrollably, Beetle squeezed her eyes shut. Despite the dragon's scorching breath and thunderous bellows, she forced herself to think logically as her parents had taught her. She reasoned that dragons belonged in fairy tales and myths. The great dinosaurs were the closest thing to dragons, and they were long extinct.

Beetle remembered feeling light-headed when she reached the dooryard. Maybe she didn't get enough oxygen when she hauled her suitcase. It could have affected her brain, somehow, and caused the horrific hallucination. She wanted her theory to be right. It was too scary to think otherwise.

Cautiously opening her eyes, Beetle breathed a sigh of relief. The dragon had been a hallucination. Making doubly certain, however, she inspected the ground for bits of wood and moss. Happily, she found none.

Still shaken by the weird experience, she rocked up on her toes, lifted the heavy iron door knocker, and let it fall. The impact made a boom that echoed throughout the inn. Beetle thought of the ruined sign and took a deep breath. She adjusted her headband, as was her habit when she was extremely nervous.

Faint vibrations inside the inn grew steadily stronger, becoming heavy footfalls.

Abruptly, the iron door latch lifted with a stiff snap, sending a ripple of apprehension across her shoulders.

When the door opened wide, Beetle craned her neck back and gaped in silence at a big woman clad in a red-and-black plaid mackinaw and bib overalls tucked into tall, green rubber boots. The crown of her blaze-orange cap barely cleared the top of the door frame.

It must be Murtha! Beetle thought. Suddenly the scolding she had feared seemed like the least of her worries. She stared blankly at the fleece-lined ear flaps jutting at odd angles from the woman's cap. Beetle's mom had said Murtha made a living as both innkeeper and hunting guide. But she hadn't told her that the woman was as big as Sasquatch!

Brushing bits of bark from her coat sleeve, the woman said, "Sorry if I kept you waiting. I was moving some firewood from the backyard to the cellar." Then she bent forward, seized Beetle's hand, and enveloped it with her oven-mitt-sized grip. Then she pumped it vigorously. "You must be Beetle Beane," she said. "I'm Murtha Bellwether. Welcome to Sooty Wick Inn."

Her head bobbling like a tin can on a stick and fearing her arm would be ripped from its socket, Beetle couldn't think straight, much less speak. She cowered as the woman drew nearer. Up close, her features magnified, Murtha looked like a huge green-eyed woodpecker.

"Why you're no bigger than a pint of cider," Murtha declared, finally letting go of Beetle's hand.

Beetle cradled her wrenched arm, quietly annoyed by Murtha's remark. After years of being called toxically cute nicknames like Small Fry, Shortcake, Smurf, and Midget by her peers, she'd become overly sensitive to comments about her small stature.

Murtha straightened. "Abel Rice got you here earlier than I expected."

The limousine had transported Beetle from Boston to the Hickory, Maine, fire station. The chauffeur had let her off there, because the car wasn't designed to handle the rough roads leading to the inn. Abel Rice, the fire chief, had taken her the rest of the way as a favor to Murtha.

Beetle bristled at the mention of the man's name. He'd chosen to drive her in an old clunky water tanker. Discarded paper cups, food wrappers, and empty foil pouches of chewing tobacco littered the floor and dashboard of the cab. She nearly choked on exhaust fumes. The engine's high whine felt like an ice pick to her brain. A mile from the station he had received a call on his radio informing him of a house fire in progress. Then a wild look came into his eyes, and he began driving the old truck like a maniac. Worst of all, when they reached the inn, he practically threw her out of the truck along with her suitcase.

Startling Beetle out of her thoughts, Murtha lifted the suitcase off the step with just one finger. "Come in," she said. Intimidated by both

8

Murtha's imposing size and strength, Beetle lingered on the step for as long as she dared. After a long minute, she worked up the nerve to enter the inn. She found herself in a cramped hall where Murtha hung her hat and coat on separate wall hooks opposite the door.

Beetle had assumed Murtha's bulky appearance was due to fat. But with the coat gone, Beetle could see that the woman was nearly all muscle.

Murtha closed the door behind Beetle and turned left.

Beetle noticed the sharp scents of candle wax, stale wood smoke, and charcoal. She kept her coat on. Judging from the inn's outer appearance, she expected the interior to be cold and dirty.

"Don't be shy. Come into the kitchen and warm up," Murtha said.

A doorway stood on either side of the hall. Beetle peeked into what looked like a large dining room to her right. Candle scones hung on dark walls. Wood beams and heavy timbers spanned the ceiling. She imagined men and women in colonial garb eating and drinking at the round tables in front of two windows facing the street. A marble bust of a man on a pedestal stood in the right corner at the back of the room, and a bar occupied the other. She was just able to see the square edge of a table at the left of the door frame.

Beetle turned and faced the doorway Murtha had entered. Her lips parted in amazement when she stepped into a high-ceilinged room where bundles of dried herbs hung from smoke-darkened beams. The room was surprisingly neat and clean, but it was nothing like the gleaming, top-of-the-line stainless-steel kitchen in her parents' posh three-story brownstone.

She advanced slowly to the center of the room and stopped in front of a pine table flanked by four mismatched chairs. The oak barrel-backed chair nearest Beetle looked specially built to accommodate Murtha's exceptional size. Lazy ribbons of steam rose from a blue-and-white enameled pot simmering on an old black cast-iron stove. Beetle inhaled the delicious aroma approvingly, despite her unease. She gazed around the room. A soapstone sink the size and shape of a horse trough caught her attention. There were no faucets, just a hand-operated pump mounted on the side. A long wooden counter stood to the right of the sink, and a white metal cabinet with a squat cylinder protruding from the top stood to its left. Beetle thought it might be an old-fashioned refrigerator.

Her eyes darted to the counter top. Surely there had to be a radio or a modern device of some kind among the tins and glass canisters. Their absence added to Beetle's eerie notion that she had stepped through the portal of a time machine and was transported back to an earlier era.

From the Stone Ledge above the Apple Bin

"This is your room." Murtha gestured toward a small room off the kitchen furnished with a twin bed nestled lengthwise against the wall opposite the door, and a night table and dresser. She placed Beetle's suitcase inside the bedroom door.

"Are you hungry?" Murtha asked.

Beetle shook her head. Even though she hadn't eaten since breakfast, she was too nervous to put anything inside her stomach.

"Come along, then," Murtha said. "I'll show you where the bathroom is."

Beetle followed Murtha around a bend in the kitchen. An enormous brick fireplace dominated the opposite wall. Three of the biggest tree mushrooms she had ever seen stood on the mantelpiece. Distracted from her fears, she thought about drawing the fascinating fan-shaped fungi, which she knew were a type of bracket mushroom.

"The bathroom is on your left," Murtha said.

Beetle reluctantly shifted her gaze away from the mushrooms, glanced at the closed bathroom door, and cringed.

After the antiquated appliances in the kitchen, she suspected the toilet was nothing more than a wooden bench with a hole in the top. She was glad she had used the restroom at the fire station before coming to the inn. At least it had bought her some time before she needed to go again.

Murtha escorted her back to the center of the kitchen. Heat radiating from both the stove and fireplace made the room feel overly warm. Beetle began to unzip her parka.

Murtha held up a wide, calloused hand. "Stop!"

Beetle's fingers froze on the zipper pull. Had Murtha finally gotten around to scolding her for damaging the sign?

Murtha rubbed her earlobe. "I'd like you to do something for me before you take off your coat."

"What is it?" Beetle asked thickly.

Murtha pulled the largest chair out from the kitchen table and sat down heavily. "Tell you in a sec." She tugged off her boots and socks, then reached beneath the table and withdrew a pair of mammoth pink bunny slippers.

Beetle gawked at the slippers. Not knowing what to make of them, she fought a rising urge to laugh.

Murtha plunged her feet into the fuzzy footwear, then wiggled her toes and bellowed like a lovesick moose. Beetle leapt back, startled. She swallowed hard, worried Murtha might have a screw loose.

Murtha rose from her chair. She stooped beside the counter, opened a cupboard door, and took out a round, wooden basket with wire handles. Beetle watched and wondered with apprehension what Murtha had in mind.

"I'd like you to go to the cellar and fill this basket with apples," Murtha said.

Beetle felt like balking at the request. The basket was big. She imagined it would be heavy when it was full. Besides, she was tired from her trip and the exertion of hauling her suitcase to the inn. However, taking into account that Murtha might be crazy, Beetle was afraid the woman could snap if she refused to help.

Beetle nodded.

Murtha directed Beetle's attention to the cellar door, then handed her the basket. "You'll find the apple bin against the back wall." She pulled a flashlight from a hip pocket in her overalls. "Take this, and be careful on the stairs."

Holding a basket handle and flashlight in her left hand, she depressed the thumb latch on the cellar door and pulled it open with her right. A sharp exhalation of cold air and the funky smell of damp earth billowed up the staircase. Standing nervously on the landing, she flicked on the flashlight. Revealing a steep set of wooden stairs, the beam punched a small bull's-eye of light through the darkness. Beetle left the door open behind her and began her descent, carefully placing her feet in hollows worn into the center of each step. Halfway down the incline, her light illuminated some unlabeled green bottles on a narrow shelf. Curious, she swiveled on her heels and studied each of the bottles. They all contained the same dark, foul-looking fluid.

Beetle wrinkled her nose and turned away. The clumsy maneuver threw her off-balance. She staggered forward, still holding the basket and flashlight. Instinctively, she threw her weight backward, hoping to break her momentum, but she lurched forward again, teetering dangerously on the edge of the step. Then, somehow, cheating gravity, she stiffened her calves, arched her back, and jammed the soles of her feet down onto the step, where they remained fixed at last.

Her breath came in quick, shallow gasps as she slumped down on the step behind her. She wiped sweat from her brow. Every cell in her body buzzed with adrenaline, and she wondered if her racing heart would ever settle down. She swallowed hard, chiding herself for letting her curiosity distract her from paying attention on the stairs.

"Are you all right?" Murtha's voice boomed from the kitchen.

The last thing Beetle wanted was for Murtha to come down the stairs and see her sorry state. "I'm fine," she answered, barely keeping the quaver out of her voice.

"Just checking," Murtha said.

Beetle sighed with relief. She ran her tongue over her bottom lip and tasted blood. She must have bitten it while teetering on the stairs. With a pang of self-pity, she thought this had to be the worst day of her life.

She missed her parents terribly, never knowing when they'd be mobilized for a mission and how long they'd be away. Even so, she supported their commitment to rescue rare and critically endangered insects under threat of imminent extinction. She felt endangered as well, staying under Murtha's roof. Sadly, there was no one to come and rescue her.

Not daring to keep Murtha waiting, she held back her tears and cautiously descended the remaining steps. She shined the light in front of her. A stone wall stood about ten feet away. Then she turned her light to the left on a small open room. A row of neatly stacked firewood stood against one wall, and a narrow set of stone steps led up to a wooden bulkhead. She abandoned the stairs reluctantly and turned right.

Already she could feel dampness creeping inside the collar of her coat. She hadn't gone far when she was startled by a looming presence with tentacles extending toward the ceiling. It took a moment for her to realize the menacing hulk was an old furnace connected to a system of overhead pipes. Freeing a hand, she drew her coat collar tightly round her neck and moved on.

She sniffed the air, relying on her sense of smell to direct her to the apple bin. The cellar broadened. Low hanging cobwebs snagged on her face and hair. She swiped at the tenacious threads, but they held like glue. Uneasy in the bowels of the inn, she hunched her shoulders. Stone pillars supporting the building's expansive underbelly came into focus. At last, her light played across a large wooden crate at the back of the cellar.

A moment later, she stood in front of the sturdy container. She shined her light inside. The apples were about a third of the way down, just beyond her reach. She placed the basket and the flashlight inside the crate. Then she hoisted her hips onto its rim and rocked forward so that her head and torso hung upside down. She extended her arms and began to fill the basket. The fruits' cloying scent was intoxicating. Her head reeled by the time she placed the last apple in the basket. She dismounted the crate and held on to its rim as she waited for her dizziness to subside.

After a moment or so, she took a deep breath and leaned forward, grasping the basket's wire handles. Straining, she managed to wrestle the basket onto the edge of the crate. As she paused to rest her arms, she heard a loud hiss. Something scythed the air a fraction from her ear. Her scream died in her throat.

Too shaken to retrieve the flashlight, she staggered back through the dark with the basket in her arms. The heavy burden slowed her progress, adding to her fear that the thing that had attacked her might strike again at any moment. After what seemed like a long time, her knees bumped painfully against something solid. She hastily explored the obstacle with her foot. She felt a vertical plane, a bump, and then a horizontal plane. She'd found the stairs.

She ascended them as quickly as she could, her feet landing helter-skelter on the worn treads. All at once, she sensed a presence racing her to the landing.

Breathless, Beetle blundered into the kitchen. Her headband had slipped down to the bridge of her nose. Half blind, she staggered about the room like a headless chicken until she tripped on her boot lace. The basket flew from her arms as she fell. The apples cascaded to the floor, pounding the floorboards, reverberating like thunder. Beetle landed, her arms and legs sprawled.

"*What in the world?*" Murtha said.

Beetle struggled onto her hands and knees in front of Murtha. She pushed her headband back into place and blurted, "I was attacked by a huge snake. It hissed and lunged at me. Its fangs just missed my head."

"A snake didn't attack you. My cat seems to be the culprit."

Beetle barely heard Murtha's words. She buried her face in her hands and choked back sobs. When she finally lifted her head, she heard a throaty growl that raised the hairs on the back of her neck. A dainty Siamese cat darted out from between Murtha's fuzzy slippers. It hissed and spat explosively at Beetle. Beetle scrambled backward, sniffling.

Murtha leaned over the defiant cat and waggled her finger. "Jezebel, you know the cellar is off limits." The cat glared at Murtha, then cowered and flattened her ears. "Apologize to Beetle for frightening her."

Beetle recoiled. "No! Keep her away from me."

Jezebel rounded on Beetle, brazenly butted her arm, and then streaked off.

Jezebel and the bunny slippers

Murtha helped Beetle stand. "Don't fret about Jezebel," Murtha said. "She'll warm up to you soon."

Beetle's stomach clenched. She took little comfort in Murtha's words.

"Let's collect the apples. Then you can take off your coat and wash up while I set the table for supper," Murtha said.

Beetle hung up her coat in the small hallway off the kitchen and headed for the bathroom. Bracing herself, she pushed open the door and was surprised to find a real toilet. Except it had a wooden water tank mounted high up on the wall behind the bowl with a long metal chain suspended from it. Smiling to herself, she guessed it had been a modern convenience back when women still wore corsets.

After operating the toilet successfully, she slid a low wooden bench out from under the sink and stood on it. She peered into the tarnished wall mirror and frowned at her thin face, hoping it would fill out soon so that she wouldn't have to go through the rest of her life looking like an elf. She whisked off her headband and shook her head vigorously to dislodge cobwebs from her dark, chin-length hair, then slid the headband back in place.

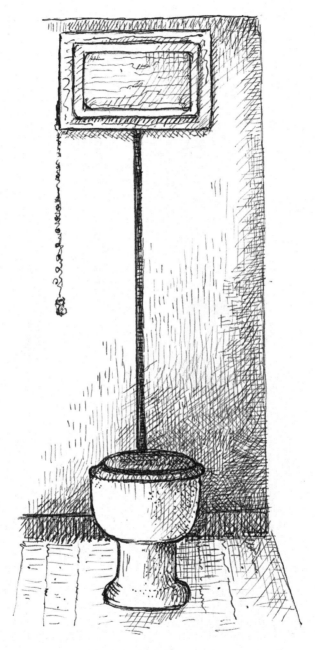

a real toilet

Ice-cold water gushed over her fingers when she turned the hot water faucet. Pipes clanked loudly in the wall behind the sink. Moments later, hot water shot from the tap. She rinsed off her hands and splashed her face, then dried herself on a hefty Murtha-size towel.

On the way back to the door, she paused beside an enormous claw-footed tub. A sizable pair of wet bloomers hung from the shower head. Beetle giggled, picturing the tub as a ship under sail with Murtha's bloomers ballooning from its mast.

peering into the tarnished mirror

Chat and Stew

Beetle's amusement faded the instant she returned to the kitchen. Eating with strangers always made her nervous. She had no idea what to talk about with Murtha. Even worse, at times like this she would often drop her silverware or spill her drink.

Murtha placed a steaming bowl of stew and a glass of milk in front of Beetle then went back to the stove. She returned with her own serving of stew in a quart-sized mixing bowl with a ladle propped inside it and sat opposite Beetle in her special chair.

Beetle tried to hide her surprise at the size of Murtha's serving. She found it even harder not to laugh when Murtha scooped up some stew with the huge long-handled spoon and drained its contents in a single gulp. After tasting the stew, Murtha pursed her lips, frowned, then reached for a full bottle of Tabasco Sauce on the table and emptied half of it into her bowl.

Beetle shook her head when Murtha tilted the bottle in her direction. She watched Murtha stir the spicy condiment into her stew and then sample it. Beetle expected to see smoke pour from the woman's ears and nose. Instead, Murtha smacked her lips, apparently unfazed by the fiery orange liquid.

Murtha removed a cloth napkin from an iron skillet in the middle of the table. "Care for some cornbread?" she asked.

Beetle eyed the golden brown squares. Their sweet aroma aroused her hunger. Despite the mass of butterflies crowding her stomach, she nodded.

Murtha placed a square of cornbread on a napkin and gave it to Beetle. Then she took two pieces for herself, slathered each one with butter, and sandwiched them together.

Beetle had been so focused on Murtha making the cornbread and butter sandwich that at first she hadn't heard the woman addressing her. She gave a self-conscious start and quickly met Murtha's gaze.

"I was just saying I miss your mom and dad. Did they tell you how we met?"

"No," Beetle said, trying to imagine what her parents could possibly have in common with this strange person. She broke off a small piece of her cornbread and nibbled it, then daintily sipped a spoonful of her stew. The combination tasted so good that she fought an urge to dunk a large chunk of her cornbread into her stew. Remembering her manners, Beetle sipped her milk politely instead. It tasted sweet and creamy, nothing like the watery skim milk Ms. Blister served at home.

"Our friendship began twelve years ago when your parents stayed at the inn while they were doing fieldwork for GIRL," Murtha explained. "It's been difficult for them to find time to visit since then, but we've kept in touch through phone calls and letters."

Beetle wondered why her parents had never mentioned Murtha to her until the previous day. She knew the acronym GIRL well. It stood for Global Insect Rescue League. Despite its name, the organization also protected rare and critically endangered spiders.

"When your mom phoned me last night, she didn't have time to explain what she and your dad will be doing in Peru." Murtha rubbed her earlobe. "Maybe you could fill me in on the details?"

Despite her shyness, Beetle had no trouble talking about her parents' mission. "They are working with a team of fellow scientists to capture as many Goldilocks spiders as possible before the Amazon River floods their habitat and then relocate them to a secret place in the Peruvian rain forest."

Murtha chuckled. "That's quite a name for a spider."

"The spiders are named after Goldilocks because of the golden hairs on their legs and abdomens. They are also the largest known ground spiders on earth–larger than a dinner plate," Beetle added. To make herself feel as if she were part of the GIRL mission, she had learned about them on the Internet the previous night.

"What caused the spiders' decline?" Murtha asked.

"Their popularity with collectors, smugglers, and importers who ignored the law protecting the rare spiders, and climate disruption."

Murtha shook her head. "That's a shame." Ladling up some stew, she went on to say, "Can the spiders save themselves by climbing trees?"

"No. They don't climb trees. They will instinctively go in their burrows to avoid the flood."

"And drown," Murtha put in.

"That's why GIRL is in such a hurry to rescue them," Beetle said.

"It sounds like your parents' mission is the spiders' only chance for survival."

Beetle nodded. Thinking aloud, she said, "I'd love to go on a GIRL mission with my parents someday." She fell into a wistful silence, doubtful her dream would ever become a reality. The missions were dangerous. Accessing rescue sites often required the team to cross deep valleys on rope bridges, hang glide off mountain-tops, and travel piranha-infested rivers in shallow dugout canoes. The team also conducted sting operations to catch criminals illegally selling rare insects. Just imagining herself taking part in any of those situations was enough to make her heart pound.

"It's just that . . . " Beetle's voice wavered. "I wouldn't be much help."

"Why's that?" Murtha asked.

"I'm not brave like my parents." Beetle instantly regretted confessing her painful secret.

"There's nothing wrong with being afraid," Murtha said, waving her ladle in the air. "Fear is a healthy response when a situation warrants it."

Beetle appreciated Murtha's point. But it did not apply to her particular problem. Fear was a constant and unwelcome presence in her life. Under its domination, she dreaded taking part in activities with other kids, because she was afraid of bungling something or making a mistake in front of them.

Embarrassed by her disclosure, Beetle fell silent and went back to eating her meal.

"A group of hunters will arrive tomorrow before sunrise," Murtha said. "I expect you to come with me mornings, when I take them to their stands. I'm back by noon, usually."

Beetle squirmed in her seat. "I'd rather stay here. I have some school assignments and a journal I'd like to work on. I brought my favorite paperbacks along, too."

Murtha didn't seem receptive to the idea. She slurped the last of her stew and slowly swirled it in her mouth before swallowing. Finally, she said, "All right. As long as you promise to stay away from the barn beside the inn. The floorboards are rotten, and the building is uninsurable, which leaves me open to a law suit if anyone gets hurt in there."

It would be an easy promise for Beetle to make. She had no interest in exploring the barn anyway. Still the thought of falling through the old flooring raised goose bumps on her arms and sent tingles up the back of her legs.

She pushed the thought from her mind and said, "I promise."

"Good." Murtha nodded with approval. "You mentioned a journal. Is it for school?"

"No. It's kind of a diary with pictures." Time flew when she wrote or sketched in her journal. It helped fill the emptiness she felt when her parents were away.

"Murtha do you have internet service?"

"No," Murtha said.

"What about cell phone service?" Beetle asked.

Murtha shook her head. "I make calls on a land line."

Beetle's spirits sunk even lower at the news that she wouldn't be able to text her best friend, Stella Piccolo.

Murtha took two more squares of cornbread from the skillet. Reaching for the butter knife, she said, "What kind of pictures?"

"Plants and animals mostly," Beetle said, growing annoyed by Murtha's questions.

After buttering both squares of cornbread and sandwiching them together, Murtha said, "Have you considered combining your interests in nature and drawing with a career in science?"

Beetle nodded. She had been considering the possibility for some time. As early as three years old she had made crayon drawings of illustrations she had found in her parents' entomology books. Her appreciation of nature had grown stronger over the years.

"You might enjoy drawing the dairy goats," Murtha said. "Their barn is at the bottom of the slope in the backyard."

"Are they friendly?" Beetle asked.

"Very," Murtha said. "You can go inside the pen with them, but remember to lock the gate behind you, or the goats will get out. Then the buck, Billy Begs, will lead the does to the barn beside the inn."

"Why?" Beetle said.

"It used to be their home before the new barn was built. Old habits die hard, I guess."

Beetle liked the idea of sketching the goats. Her stay at the inn might not be as boring as she had feared. Excited by the prospect, she finished her meal. Then a disturbing thought dampened her enthusiasm. Murtha's goats enjoyed the comforts of food and shelter, unlike wild deer that had to sustain themselves and contend with the annual onslaught of hunters.

When it came to hunting, Beetle sided with the deer. She wondered how unarmed hunters would feel if gun-toting deer chased them through the woods. She didn't dare share the notion with Murtha. The next instant, she surprised herself by blurting, "I don't think hunting is fair to deer. Hunters have all the advantages." Beetle tensed, fearing her comments might provoke Murtha's wrath.

Murtha finished her cornbread and butter sandwich in three bites. Licking her fingers, she gazed intently at Beetle, her expression unreadable. "Deer are not as vulnerable as you might think," she said. "Their keen senses and speed give them considerable advantages over hunters."

Murtha's unruffled response was a welcome relief to Beetle. Moreover, she was pleased to learn that deer were good at evading hunters."

Murtha furrowed her brow. "I gather you don't like hunting."

Beetle nodded cautiously.

"Do you know any hunters?"

"No," Beetle said. Nor did she want to.

"I hope you won't find it difficult to be around the hunters. Their company will be unavoidable at times, especially during meals. I think you will find them to be a friendly lot in spite of your misgivings. None of them would take a deer's life for frivolous reasons. I know because I screen my clients carefully."

Beetle had listened politely. But she doubted the hunters possessed any redeeming qualities. As she gazed down at her empty bowl, it occurred to her that the meat in the stew might have been venison. She should have thought to ask Murtha before she had eaten it. Her lack of mindfulness made her feel like a hypocrite. She resolved to pay closer attention to what Murtha served in the future.

Murtha got up and cleared the table. Standing at the sink, she glanced over her shoulder and said, "Beetle, can you handle a paring knife?"

Beetle hesitated to answer. She had no cooking experience. Lydia Blister prepared all the meals for the family, and she would not allow anyone to help her in the kitchen. But Beetle had dissected an earthworm with a small scalpel in biology class once. That had to count for something. Reluctantly, she said, "Yes."

After placing the basket of apples on the table, Murtha gave Beetle a paring knife, a wooden cutting board, and a large stainless steel bowl. Then she sat across from Beetle, equipped with a paring knife and a large stainless steel bowl of her own.

"You slice; I'll peel and core," she said, plucking an apple from the basket.

Murtha plied her knife, turning the apple round and round. An unbroken peel rapidly descended from her large hands into the metal bowl. After expertly separating the apple from its skin, she made several quick incisions, extracted the core, and placed it on Beetle's cutting board. "I prefer half-inch slices for my pies," she instructed.

Holding the apple on the cutting board, Beetle inserted the knife into the fruit's flesh. Then she pressed down with the blade, accidentally jabbing a finger. The apple juice made the cut sting like fire, but a discreet glance revealed it was just a tiny nick, too shallow to draw blood. After about five laborious minutes, Beetle assessed the lopsided apple wedges, scattered higgledy-piggledy across the cutting board, and concluded she could not have done worse blindfolded. Tilting the cutting board to obscure Murtha's view, she dumped the wedges into her bowl.

Murtha glanced at the contents of Beetle's bowl as she set a second apple on the cutting board.

Beetle shrank into her seat, expecting Murtha to criticize the way she had sliced the apple. Despite her determination not to like Murtha, she inexplicably craved the woman's approval.

"Would you do something for me while I'm out with the men tomorrow?" Murtha asked.

Beetle blinked away her confusion as she realized that Murtha hadn't faulted her on her handling of the paring knife, but had asked for a favor instead. The last time she did something for Murtha, she'd nearly broken her neck on the cellar stairs.

"Jezebel has a habit of opening the cellar door and sneaking downstairs to hunt mice. "If she catches one and it eats it, she vomits it up. I put Jezebel in her room with a litter box when I leave the inn. She hates being confined, but it's for her own good," Murtha said.

Beetle listened, wondering why Murtha was going on about Jezebel.

"Since you'll be here anyway," Murtha continued. "I thought Jezebel could enjoy some freedom."

A tight ball of discomfort formed in the pit of Beetle's stomach. *Jezebel hated her. Murtha had to be blind not to have noticed.* Beetle's inexplicable urge to please the woman vanished.

"Do I have to watch her all the time?" she asked.

"No. All you have to do is make sure the latch on the door is secure. You can check it by pulling the door handle. If the door stays closed, you know the bar on the opposite side of the door is seated in its cradle," Murtha said.

Beetle pursed her lips. She didn't make promises lightly. When she gave her word, she always kept it. She wanted the beastly cat to be confined; there was no telling what she might get up to with Murtha away. But as Murtha's guest how could say no?

Meeting Murtha's Ancestors

The grandfather clock in the hall chimed nine times.

"Good heavens," Murtha said. "It's getting late. You had better turn in, Beetle." She stood up from the kitchen table. "I hope you don't mind sharing a bed with Jezebel."

Beetle's eyes widened with alarm. Still annoyed that she had reluctantly agreed to check the latch on the cellar door so that Jezebel could move freely about the inn, Beetle resisted the proposed sleeping arrangement. Surprising herself, she blurted, "I'd rather stand inside a broom closet all night than share a bed with her."

"Jezebel's bedroom is the best I can do." Murtha shrugged. "This is my busiest time."

"Can Jezebel sleep with you instead?" Beetle asked.

Murtha shook her head. "Jezebel won't give up her room."

"Can I sleep in one of the empty rooms upstairs?" Beetle asked.

"No. Those rooms are reserved for the hunters. They will want to stow their gear in their rooms as soon as they arrive."

Beetle noticed that Murtha's patience sounded strained. She suddenly came to the painful realization that she had been thinking only of herself. Clearly, Murtha had enough to do without catering to the demands of a selfish brat. Embarrassed, she ceased her complaining and stared down at the floor. Tears pricked the back of her eyes.

"On second thought," Murtha said. "The grand room is available."

Beetle looked up and smiled for the first time since she had arrived. *Wow, the grand room,* she thought. "Can I see it, please?"

"Sure," Murtha said. "You can meet some of my ancestors while you're at it."

The joy drained from Beetle's smile. Could the grand room be a shrine to Murtha's dead ancestors? She pictured rows of urns bearing their ashes lined up on shelves. Preferring, however, to believe the room was as magnificent as its name suggested, she quickly dismissed the notion. Murtha ushered Beetle into the front hallway past another entrance to the dining room. Jezebel skulked at their heels as they rounded the base of a wide staircase and then stopped in front of a closed door.

Beetle's heart pounded with anticipation. Murtha opened the door and flicked on a switch, illuminating a bank of dusty crystal chandeliers. Broadly sweeping an arm, she said, "Everything in here is original with the exception of electricity."

Beetle frowned as she surveyed the room's interior. It was grand in scale, bigger than both the kitchen and the dining room put together. However, it was nothing like she had imagined. It was as stuffy as a Pharaoh's tomb, and a thick layer of dust carpeted the expansive parquet floor. Spider webs looped between the chandeliers like crepe paper garlands. Adding to its neglected appearance, the room was unfurnished except for a dozen or so folded cots.

"The grand room was a banquet hall once," Murtha explained. "Erasmus Bellwether had it built when the inn became a stage coach stop. He thought it would attract affluent guests. But the room turned out to be a huge flop. Erasmus would turn over in his grave if he knew I was using it as a dormitory for hunters when the inn is filled to capacity."

As Beetle stared into the empty marble fireplace on the opposite side of the room, an unbidden image of Erasmus spinning restlessly in his grave entered her mind. Disillusioned by the state of the room, she turned abruptly to encounter a dozen gilt-framed portraits mounted on a white-paneled wall. A spidery tingle crept up her spine.

"These portraits represent the earliest members of the Bellwether family," Murtha said proudly. Starting with the first painting on the right, she began naming each ancestor aloud: "Peregrine, Melville, Aldrich, Lindisfarn, Gretna, Philemon, Zilpah, Lizzie, Bazaleel, Chauncey, Templeton, and Smyrna."

The Bellwethers' pale faces glowed with ghostly incandescence against the dark backgrounds in each of their paintings, making them look as if they belonged in a chamber of horrors. All of Murtha's ancestors appeared normal in height. So where had Murtha's imposing stature come from? Beetle wanted to know, but she didn't dare ask.

Unable to bear their glowering countenances a moment longer, Beetle informed Murtha that she would be sleeping in Jezebel's room after all, then rushed out the door.

Jezebel streaked past Beetle in the hallway, entered the kitchen first, and then skittered into her room.

Arrested by a pair of eyes glowing like icy lanterns in the dark, Beetle froze in the doorway to Jezebel's room. A low, undulating growl sent a chill up her spine. Frantically running her hand over the bedroom wall close to the door frame, she managed to find a light switch and flicked it on. Light flooded the room to expose Jezebel crouched on the twin bed. The cat dug her sharp, scimitar-shaped claws into the coverlet, scowling like a samurai warrior.

Beetle yelped and took a step back. She'd finally had enough of the weird giantess and her evil companion. Fleeing the inn was all that mattered now. She attempted a hasty retreat. Murtha's solid body thwarted her escape. The bone-jarring collision left Beetle dazed. Before she could recover her wits, Murtha grasped her shoulders and propelled her into the bedroom.

"Let go of me!" Beetle demanded, digging in her heels. Helpless to free herself from Murtha's vice-like grip, she advanced farther into the room. As she came close to the bed, Jezebel spat, her body tensed and ready to spring.

Her heart racing, Beetle recoiled and crossed her arms over her face. Seconds passed without the ferocious cat launching a strike.

Beetle cautiously peeked out from beneath her arms. Amazingly, Jezebel lay cowering on the coverlet, her gaze apparently fixed on Murtha.

Beetle wondered if Murtha had extinguished Jezebel's fiery disposition with a silent command.

Just then Jezebel slinked off the bed and crouched by the door. Beetle finally felt safe enough to lower her arms. Exhausted, she slouched onto the edge of the bed. Murtha sat down beside her.

Beetle pulled away from Murtha. "I want to go home!" she said hotly.

"You know that isn't possible," Murtha said.

It was true. Beetle grew even angrier. She realized how powerless she was. "Why did you make me go into the room when Jezebel was threatening to attack me?" Beetle's chest heaved with outrage. Staring at Murtha, she waited for an explanation.

"I'm sorry you were frightened. I pushed you into the room knowing Jezebel would back down. It was important for you to see that her aggressive behavior is just an act. Now that you have met her bluff, she won't bother you again."

Beetle did not find Murtha's words reassuring. In fact, she couldn't help wondering if the woman shared a sadistic streak with Jezebel. Tears leaked from her eyes as she stared accusingly at her tormentor, still huddled by the bedroom door.

"Jezebel is a bully," she blurted. "I haven't done anything to her. Why is she being so horrible to me?"

"I think you should hear Jezebel's story," Murtha said. "It might help you understand why she behaves badly toward strangers. First, I'll fix you a hot chocolate to calm your nerves."

Murtha stood up and said, "Come Jezebel. Beetle needs some time to herself."

Jezebel followed her mistress into the kitchen. Soon, the teakettle let out a sharp whistle. A few minutes later, Murtha returned with a mug of hot chocolate and a bunch of Kleenex. She gave Beetle the Kleenex first and said, "Dry your eyes."

Beetle blew her nose and mopped her face. When she felt confident that her involuntary shudders had passed, she accepted the mug and set it on her lap beside the soggy wad of Kleenex. Murtha sat gently on the bed without disturbing the mug of chocolate on Beetle's lap.

Jezebel slinked back into the room and sat on her haunches.

Beetle glared at her. She doubted anything Murtha was about to say could change her opinion of Jezebel. She took a sip of hot chocolate. It tasted delicious, and the dollop of whipped cream on top tickled her nose. She suppressed a smile, determined to maintain her sullen expression.

Apparently satisfied that Beetle had settled down, Murtha began the story. "A snowplow driver brought Jezebel to my door on a frigid night five years ago. He found her in a burlap sack, lying on a snow bank. She had hypothermia and barely any meat on her bones. I fed her warm milk with an eyedropper and put her in a basket near the stove." Murtha's eyes misted. "I didn't think she would survive the night. But she was wide awake and hungry the next morning."

"Jezebel looks healthy enough today," Murtha continued. "But she still bears the emotional scars from her ordeal. As a result, she needs to feel in control around strangers."

Beetle could understand how Jezebel's abandonment had made her distrustful of strangers. Her resentment toward Jezebel softened, but still she resolved to keep up her guard until the cat proved she could be trusted.

She drank the last of her hot chocolate and savored the rich sediment at the bottom of the mug.

Murtha took the empty mug from Beetle and asked, "Do you have the flashlight you took to the cellar?"

"No. I dropped it when Jezebel frightened me," Beetle said, worried Murtha might ask her to go back in the dank, dark cellar and retrieve it.

"I'll get you another one," Murtha said as if she'd sensed Beetle's concern. She left the room.

Beetle heard a drawer open in the kitchen. A moment later Murtha returned with a flashlight. "The power goes out a lot around here. Keep this light on your bedside table. It will come in handy if there's a power failure and you need to get up at night. There are extra batteries and flashlights in the left-hand drawer in the counter."

Jezebel claimed the head of the bed as soon as Murtha left the room to make pies. Watching Jezebel closely for any signs of a surprise attack, Beetle put on her flannel pajamas. Seeing none, she approached the bed slowly and cautiously peeled back the covers.

Still unopposed by Jezebel, Beetle eased herself onto the edge of the bed and lay stiffly on her side.

Gradually raising the covers to her chin, she half expected Jezebel's sharp nails to rake her back at any moment. The cat suddenly dove under the covers and tunneled toward the foot board. Beetle jerked her legs to her chest, prepared to leap out of bed at the least sign of more trouble.

Exhausted from the trying events of the day, Beetle mustered the nerve to turn off the lamp on the bedside table, then slowly stretched out her legs before rolling onto her back.

Cloves and cinnamon scented the dark room. Beetle breathed in the exotic aroma and listened to alternating squeaks and thuds emanating from the kitchen.

It took a moment for her to connect the sounds with the back and forth motion of Murtha's rolling pin flattening dough. The hypnotic cadence made her drowsy. The last thing she felt before drifting off to sleep was Jezebel curled comfortably by her bare feet.

The Color Orange

Beetle awoke to the sound of truck doors slamming and muffled voices drifting toward the inn in the early morning darkness. She blearily checked her alarm clock: 4:30 AM. Stumbling out of bed, she peered through the partly open door. Six men entered the bright kitchen and leaned their black powder muskets against the wall nearest the kitchen door. Their presence seemed to fill the room.

Three of the hunters were young, tall, and lanky. Clad in fluorescent orange coveralls, they reminded Beetle of overgrown carrots. The other three men, gray-haired and wearing caps and jackets of faded orange, looked like seasoned hunters.

Murtha spoke to the three carrot men first, then introduced them to the other hunters. Vigorous handshakes ensued, and Murtha gave each of the men a numbered room key. Beetle lost sight of the hunters as they carried their gear toward the front hall. The inn's timbers shook as the men pounded up the stairs. Then the floorboards creaked overhead as they went to their assigned rooms.

After a short time, the hunters returned to the kitchen with their backpacks. The older-looking men removed their thermoses from their backpacks and filled them with coffee from a large urn on the kitchen counter. The younger men followed suit. Then the hunters each took several plastic-wrapped sandwiches from a large platter beside the coffee urn and placed them in their backpacks along with their thermoses.

The jovial mood in the room turned serious when Murtha put on her plaid mackinaw, orange vest, and hunting cap. Silently shrugging on their backpacks, the men took up their muskets and followed Murtha out the door.

Beetle hurried to the kitchen and peeked out a window. She saw Murtha squeeze her large frame into the Volkswagen bus, causing it to sag on its springs. Adding to the bus's strain, a hunter got in beside her. The vehicle sagged even further when the rest of the men piled in the side door.

The bus's engine sputtered to life, and the old rattletrap trundled down the driveway into the thinning darkness.

Murtha and the hunters had been gone for three hours. Beetle had already eaten breakfast and checked the latch on the cellar door. She could hardly wait to sketch the goats in the backyard. Beckoned by soft November sun, she put on her coat, took the apple scraps she had pilfered from the kitchen sink and bundled in a dish towel earlier that morning, and tucked the package in her coat pocket.

She was just about to pick up her journal and pens from the kitchen table when she noticed the laces on one of her boots had come undone. She bent over to fix it. Just as Beetle finished tying the knot, she glimpsed Jezebel streaking through the open cellar door. Beetle had tested the latch. Why hadn't it held? The only explanation she could think of was she hadn't checked it properly.

"Jezebel! Come back!" Beetle shouted as she ran for the flashlight on the bedside table. The big breakfast she'd eaten suddenly felt like a cement block in her stomach. She descended the treacherous cellar stairs as quickly as she dared. Standing on the bottom step, she shouted, "Jezebel, where are you?" She panned the light from left to right.

Suddenly Jezebel shot out from behind the old furnace and scurried through a gap under a wooden door set in the foundation.

Beetle leapt off the bottom step and chased after the cat. Reaching the door, she dropped onto her stomach and aimed the flashlight through the narrow opening. Jezebel peered back, her eyes shining eerily.

"Come out of there," Beetle demanded.

Grinning like the Cheshire Cat, Jezebel remained in a crouched position. Beetle slid her hand under the door in an effort to rouse the cat. Jezebel backed away.

Beetle withdrew her hand and pushed herself up onto her knees, then sat back on her heels and huffed. Now she would have to find Jezebel and bring her back up the stairs to the inn.

Rising stiffly from her cramped position, Beetle tucked the flashlight under her arm. Then she wiped her gritty hands on her dirt-streaked jeans and grasped the rusty door handle. She hesitated for an instant as she pictured a crypt on the other side of the door, a crypt where the bones of Murtha's ancestors were interred. Pushing the morbid thought to the back of her mind, she thumbed the latch and pulled. The door held fast as it chafed against its frame.

Beetle braced her feet on the floor and pulled again, harder this time. The door broke free and opened with a loud *crack*, nearly causing her to fall over backward. She shined the light inside the opening. A wave of chill air, stinking of moldy spinach, bit the back of Beetle's throat. There was no sign of the errant cat nor the skeletons she'd half expected to spill out of the dark cavity.

Bewildered by Jezebel's disappearance, she inspected the inside of what appeared to be a wooden storage closet with a dirt floor. There was no indication as to how Jezebel had accomplished her vanishing act.

Beetle heard a grating sound and started. She looked over her shoulder. It was only the closet door closing. She studied the walls and floor again, then realized there was no ceiling. Beetle felt a thrill, confident the cat must be hiding on the framework surrounding the top of the closet. She faced the back wall, leaned her weight against it, and rocked up on her toes. Stretching, she shined the light above her head.

The wall juddered seconds before it gave way. There was no time to save herself. The thin, chill air seemed to hasten her fall. She landed on a dirt floor in pitch-darkness. The wall slammed back into place behind her with a loud snick. It sounded like a lock slotting into place.

The impact rattled her bones, forcing the wind from her lungs. She lay sprawled on her stomach, her cheek squashed against the dirt floor. Each unsuccessful attempt to draw breath caused excruciating pain in her chest. Afraid she might never breathe again, she kept her eyes closed. Finally, her lifeless lungs swelled with air. Flooded with relief, she opened her watery eyes. A blurred light caught her attention. She stretched her arm toward the flashlight and closed her hand around it. From what she could tell, the ground beneath her seemed level with the closet floor.

The solidity of the flashlight provided her with a scrap of comfort.

Beetle cautiously moved her legs, then wiggled her shoulders and hips. Aside from the tenderness in her ribs, nothing felt broken. Confused and afraid, she slowly propped herself up on her elbows and grimly observed her surroundings with the flashlight. She seemed to be in a small room. Rough stone walls loomed on either side of her. Long, wiry roots hung down between stone slabs in the ceiling. One of the roots jerked upward forming a U shape and then slithered into a crevice high up on the wall. A few seconds passed before Beetle realized the animated root was actually a snake. She inhaled sharply and flinched. Normally she liked snakes, but the reptile's unexpected appearance in this dark, confining place scared the wits out of her.

In the dead silence, she could hear only her blood pounding in her ears. She rolled frantically onto her back and sat up. Desperate to find a way out, she shined her light on the backside of the trick wall. Though she knew little about construction, she could see that the wall wasn't a wall at all but a cleverly disguised door. The secret entrance inside the closet had been built for a purpose. Beetle dared not think about what it might be.

On further inspection she could not find a latch of any kind. Sweat broke out on her forehead.

What if the door only opened from the outside?

The thought of imprisonment in this stone vault gripped her heart. What if she were to scream for help and no one came to let her out? The answer came unbidden: She would die. Overcome by a sense of doom, she envisioned herself rationing the apple peelings in her pocket in hopes of staying alive as long as the oxygen held out in the room.

Beetle pushed the notion out of her mind. Fear wasn't helping her situation any. After achieving a small degree of calm, it occurred to her to break down the door. Sitting firmly on her backside, she braced her arms by her sides, drew both legs to her chest, and forcefully kicked the door.

It flew open with little resistance.

She hadn't expected it to swing in both directions. When it slammed shut almost instantly, she heard the same faint snick. This time she knew it was just a harmless catch. Something between a sob and a laugh burst from her throat. She would easily be able to return to the cellar.

Beetle tottered to her feet with the intention of going back to the storage closet through the secret door. It would be easy to find Jezebel now that she knew where to look for her. Then she would coax the cat down with some Chowcat salmon-flavored crunchies she had seen Jezebel gobble up the previous night. Thinking of all the trouble she could have saved herself, Beetle wished she had thought of luring Jezebel out of the closet with food in the first place.

She was about to leave the moldy little dungeon when she suddenly heard a nearby meow. Turning toward the cry, Beetle discovered she had been in a tunnel all along. As far as she could tell it was about four feet wide and seven feet tall.

Just then, Jezebel let out a bloodcurdling wail that sent a shiver up Beetle's spine.

More than anything, Beetle wanted to leave the cold, dank place. But she had to find Jezebel.

She checked the tunnel walls, roof, and floor with her flashlight before daring to take another step. Satisfied that it looked safe but uncertain of her destination, she ventured forward.

She drew her coat collar tight to her neck just in case there were more snakes dangling from the ceiling. Cold silence met her frequent calls to Jezebel. In places, water seeped out of the stonework. She gasped and nearly dropped the flashlight when a rat streaked across her path. The skeletal creature looked as if it hadn't eaten in a long time. Beetle's skin crawled. Was there a pack of rats as ravenous-looking as this one up ahead? She immediately thought of Jezebel's anguished cry. Could they have gotten her?

Sickened by the notion, Beetle slumped against a wall. The slant of her light illuminated a lizard-like creature inches from her right cheek. She jerked upright and whirled around. Something about its appearance jogged her memory. Her alarm quickly subsided, giving way to scientific curiosity. After a few passes with the light she found the creature on the wall again. Large yellow dots contrasted sharply against its shiny black body. Just as she had thought, it was a yellow spotted salamander.

a lizard-like creature

With a jolt, she snapped out of her fascination with the salamander. How could she have let her curiosity distract her from the serious matter at hand?

Once more chill air wrapped around her like an invisible film. She pressed her lips in a determined line as she pushed on through the tunnel. Beetle hoped that Jezebel was alive and unharmed.

Soon Beetle came to a brick archway and cautiously stepped through the opening, then panned the light around. A cavernous cellar dominated by a huge earthen ramp reinforced by stone retaining walls yawned before her. The ramp reminded her of the approach to a castle.

It began on the left about ten feet from a pair of wide double doors set into the foundation. From there the ramp gained height as it gradually formed a long U shape that disappeared inside a recess in the ceiling.

Beetle guessed it was used to move large animals in and out of a building. Shifting her attention from the ramp, she called to Jezebel. There was no response.

Beetle frowned. Why didn't Jezebel show herself or at least meow?

Shoulders hunched against the chill, Beetle turned to her right and walked along the stone foundation. Her patience suddenly worn thin, she stamped her foot and shouted, "Jezebel I've had enough of your games." She hadn't expected a response from the cat, but she let out a sob just the same.

Barely containing her emotions, Beetle paused, then plodded on. Spider webs snapped against her face as she progressed through the cellar. Her feet stirred up dust from hay chaff littering the dirt floor. She suddenly sneezed. A violent gust came out of her mouth as a loud hoot. Her head and eyeballs felt scrambled. When Beetle's head cleared, she resumed her search. She halted where the back of the foundation merged with the ramp.

Beetle's breath caught in her throat. At her feet lay a gnawed and moldering animal skeleton. The remains suggested the animal had been about the size of a cat. Had it died of natural causes? Or had the culprit been another animal or possibly a pack of animals that frequented the cellar? Her contempt for Jezebel immediately turned to concern. She wondered if the horde of starving rats she had imagined in the tunnel existed. If they did, maybe Murtha's cat was already dead, chewed to pieces like the remains before her. She feared for a second time that Jezebel's life could be in peril.

Beetle hurried back the way she had come and then followed the foundation around the other side of the ramp. After finding no sign of Jezebel, Beetle scrambled up the ramp. It led to a landing where she found a wide doorway with a length of old burlap nailed across the top of the frame.

The flashlight beam dimmed, then went out, leaving her in complete darkness. She thumbed the switch. Nothing happened.

She tried not to panic as she slowly unscrewed the flashlight lens. The instant it came free, she felt batteries shoot out. A second later, she heard them hit the ground and roll down the ramp. Her stomach knotted with frustration. She tried to reassemble the flashlight, but her efforts failed.

"One more thing to go wrong," she grumbled, stuffing the useless light into her coat pocket.

She hesitated in front of the doorway. Part of her dreaded what she might encounter beyond the burlap curtain, and another part doubted it could be any worse than what she'd already been through. Taking a deep breath, she probed the air with her fingers until they brushed against the coarse cloth she had seen. Its musty smell engulfed her as she pushed it aside, and she released an unexpected avalanche of dust that stung her throat and eyes.

Dim, grainy light painted the narrow room beyond the doorway. She was glad there was enough light to make up for the useless flashlight.

Beetle squinted into the gloom.

Her spirits rose as she spotted Jezebel's shadowy form framed off to the right by an entrance large enough to accommodate an elephant performing a headstand. Jezebel sat still until Beetle drew within arm's reach of her.

Then the fickle cat turned and bounded through the opening. "Don't you dare run off again," Beetle shouted, scurrying after the cat.

Pale shafts of light slanted down from a row of small windows above a tall door to her left. From what she could see, Beetle guessed she had followed Jezebel into the forbidden barn.

Recalling Murtha's warning about rotten floorboards, Beetle froze where she was standing. A chill shot up the back of her legs. She reflected on how lucky she'd been to have made it thus far without crashing through the floor.

In spite of her frightening realization, she couldn't turn back. She'd been through too much to give up on finding Jezebel. After all, how could she face Murtha if she lost the cat?

She carefully tested the next floorboard with her foot before daring to put her full weight on it. Repeating the process, she inched along as Jezebel slipped farther into the dark recesses of the barn.

The air felt much warmer than in the tunnel. It smelled of musk and damp fur. Beetle strained to see, waiting for her eyes to adjust to muted light. Indistinct shadows shifted in and out of steamy haze. She inhaled sharply as the shadows gradually took form.

Blinking, she looked again to make sure her eyes hadn't deceived her.

She'd been right the first time.

There were at least a dozen deer in there.

Her mind raced as she struggled to process the unexpected sight when a magnificent white buck strode into the shafts of light lent by the small windows above the door to her left.

His broad, forked antlers looked like limbs of a mighty oak. Beetle's wonderment quickly turned to fear. She realized the buck seemed agitated by her presence.

She tried to back out of the room, but the buck darted around her. Beetle wheeled and backed up as, antlers lowered, he advanced on her until she could not move. With her back pressed against a wall, she thought she might faint from fright.

The buck's fiery red irises made him look like a hellish demon. Powerful muscles in his neck twitched beneath his snowy white hide. He could easily run her through with his sharp antlers.

Assuming the slightest movement on her part could provoke an attack, she tried to stand perfectly still. But she could not keep her face from contorting into a tight grimace as the buck inhaled sharply through flared nostrils. She watched, transfixed, as he curled his upper lip over his nostrils and tilted his head back as if deliberately making a funny face.

Beetle would have laughed if she hadn't been so terrified. It occurred to her that he might be testing her scent to determine whether she presented a threat. She could hear her parka's metal zipper pull clicking back and forth in time with her frantic heartbeats.

After what seemed an eternity, the buck unfurled his lip and tipped his head forward again. His pupils contracted and his irises softened, changing from fiery red to silver star bursts with pinkish centers. The buck nodded vigorously and stepped back.

It took Beetle a minute to realize that she had gained his acceptance. She shuddered out a breath. Feeling tension drain away, she took a few steps forward.

Her eyes focused on the buck, she slowly removed the bundle of apple scraps she had tucked into her pocket earlier that morning.

The buck appeared interested and offered no threat. She unfolded the bundle, selected the biggest apple core, and presented it to him.

striding into shafts of light

She could feel his chin hairs tickle her palm as he sniffed the core before gently coaxing it into his mouth. He chomped on the apple core and stepped aside as if to grant her access to the herd.

Beetle felt privileged to be accepted by the buck. As she approached the does, they raised their pointed snouts and sniffed the air, apparently aroused by the scent of apples. Mobbed within seconds by the deer, Beetle feared she would be crushed by their jostling bodies. The does craned their slender necks and stuck out their long, dexterous tongues to extend their reach toward the bundle of scraps. Beetle could feel hot deer breath on her cheeks and down the back of her neck. Two fawns tugged at the bundle. She yanked it away just in time.

Desperate to escape the melée, she clutched the deers' coveted prize to her chest and drew a deep breath before slowly pushing her way through the throng of does and fawns. They made way for her, then quickly settled down as she scattered apple scraps on the floor. Beetle did not blame the deer for nearly squashing her in their attempt to get a share of the fruit. Despite her fear, she had found the experience strangely exhilarating. As she admired their beautiful red coats and willowy frames, she wondered how they had come to be in the dark, stuffy barn.

Then she tucked the dish towel into her coat pocket and sat down on a hay bale to think.

Her head whirled with questions about the secret door at the back of the storage closet, the weird tunnel, and Murtha's making Beetle promise to stay away from the barn because of the rotten floorboards. The floor had easily supported her weight. She suspected it was a lie to keep her from finding the deer.

The possibility made her question Murtha's honesty and her motives for confining the deer. A sickening thought that Murtha raised the deer for meat and sold it on the black market entered her mind. Another equally gruesome thought occurred to her. Maybe Murtha provided deer to hunters who came to the inn. She pictured hunters waiting outside the barn door, guns ready, for Murtha to release the deer to a barrage of gunfire.

Beetle shuddered. Either way, the deer would face a premature death.

She suppressed an urge to let the deer out of the barn. Caution told her not to interfere until she was able to determine the truth.

Suddenly aware that light slanting into the barn had brightened considerably, Beetle snapped out of her troubled reverie. How long had she been sitting on the hay bale thinking? For all she knew, it might be noon already! She still had to find Jezebel, return to the inn, and change her clothes before Murtha returned. Otherwise, her grubby appearance could lead to difficult questions about how she'd spent her morning.

She scrambled to her feet and called to Jezebel one last time. When the cat did not present herself, Beetle dreaded having to tell Murtha she had failed to keep Jezebel from sneaking into the cellar. But she couldn't delay returning to the inn much longer.

The thought of going back through the tunnel without a working flashlight made her shiver. She considered leaving through the big door at the back of the barn, but ruled it out because the deer might run away when she opened it.

Then she spotted a waist-high window in the narrow room beyond the huge opening.

Unchallenged, Beetle walked past the white buck. She went to the window and pushed up on the sash. When it held fast, she pushed even harder. Just as she thought her strength would give out, the window came unstuck with a loud snap, shaking loose a flurry of desiccated fly carcasses. She hoisted herself onto the narrow sill, turned awkwardly on her knees, and slowly backed out the window. Her feet had barely touched the ground when Jezebel appeared on the windowsill and brushed her cheek against Beetle's shoulder.

Beetle suspected Jezebel was trying to charm her way out of a scolding. But she was so pleased to see the cat that a rebuke was the farthest thing from her mind. She quickly scooped Jezebel up into her arms and hurried back to the inn.

Putting on a Brave Front

Beetle said little during lunch, pretending nothing out of the ordinary had happened that morning. When the meal ended, she hurried to her room, eager to read *The Case of the Missing Swan*, hoping to get some pointers from her favorite girl detective, Greta Spleen. Absorbed in the book, she jumped when the teakettle whistled shrilly from the kitchen.

"You've been in your room most of the afternoon," Murtha said as she stood outside the bedroom doorway. "Come out and have a mug of hot chocolate."

Beetle felt irritated by the interruption, but she knew it would be rude to refuse Murtha's invitation. She reluctantly went to the kitchen and sat at the table. Murtha placed a mug of hot chocolate in front of her. "Thanks," Beetle said, hoping to put in a brief appearance and then go back to her room.

Murtha went to the stove and began shifting pots and pans. She returned shortly, carrying a large bowl of boiled potatoes and a metal potato masher. Then she sat down opposite Beetle.

Her face flushed from preparing the evening meal, Murtha looked at Beetle and said, "Are you feeling all right? You were very quiet at lunch."

Murtha's query worried Beetle. "I'm fine," she said, attempting to sound as if nothing was bothering her.

"*Good.* Then I expect you to come with me tomorrow morning. This is supposed to be your vacation. You should be out in the fresh air instead of doing homework."

Beetle tensed. Why had Murtha suddenly changed her mind about letting her stay at the inn alone? Did Murtha suspect she had discovered the deer? If so, how close was she to figuring it out? Beetle's stomach squirmed like a sack of eels under Murtha's scrutiny. There was no point in protesting. Clearly she had no choice in the matter. "All right," she said.

In *The Case of the Deadly Decoy,* Beetle remembered Greta Spleen brilliantly turning a hopeless situation to her advantage. It occurred to Beetle that she could do the same thing. By accompanying Murtha, she could find out whether the woman was serious about being a hunting guide or if she just used the job title as a cover for illegal activities. Searching for any signs that the woman possessed a criminal mind, she stole a furtive glance at Murtha.

The masher looked like a toy in Murtha's grapefruit-sized fist. Beetle raised her mug as Murtha plunged the utensil into the bowl. She was certain the force of the impact would rock the table and send her drink sloshing over the rim. Still holding the mug in the air, Beetle slid back in her chair and tensed each time Murtha delivered a crushing blow with the masher. In a matter of seconds, Murtha had reduced the potatoes to a pulpy mass. She rapped the masher against the side of the bowl and said, "Beetle, what happened to the apple peelings that were in the sink?"

Alarm bells went off in Beetle's head. Was Murtha making casual conversation or was she doing some sleuthing of her own? She disliked lying, but she couldn't tell Murtha the truth. Beetle hastily swallowed a mouthful of cocoa and accidentally inhaled it while trying to come up with a credible response. As she gasped for air, cocoa shot out her nostrils. Embarrassed, she mopped her face with a napkin as she struggled to bring her coughing fit under control.

"Do you need a slap on the back?" Murtha asked.

Beetle shook her head. Suddenly she had an idea. After catching her breath, she blurted, "I . . . fed the apple peelings to the goats."

"Oh," Murtha said. "I'm sure the goats were very appreciative. Did you make drawings of them?"

Beetle blinked hard. When the explanation had popped into her head, she hadn't thought about pictures—proof of how she had spent her morning. She had to think fast. If she answered no, she could open herself to more questions about her activities that morning. Impulsively she said, "Yes." Then hastily added, "But they are not finished yet."

"I'd like to see them when they're done," Murtha said.

Beetle nodded, hiding her unease. Her answer was only a temporary fix. She resolved to make some sketches of the goats after she had a chance to observe them in person, partly to make up for the lie and partly out of principle.

Murtha carried the bowl and masher to the counter. She added butter, milk, and seasonings to the mashed potatoes, then vigorously blended the contents with a long-handled wooden spoon. After covering the bowl with a large pot lid, she went to the hall off the kitchen and put on her coat and hat.

Beetle nervously bit her lip as she watched Murtha leave. She felt wrung out from their conversation. More than anything, she wanted to know what was on the woman's mind.

That evening, Beetle reluctantly joined Murtha and the hunters for supper in the dining room. A brilliant blaze in the fireplace illuminated the table, in sharp contrast with the dimly lit room.

Beetle's headband pinched her scalp, reminding her unnecessarily that she was nervous around strangers. She darted glances at the hunters, wondering whether they had come to hunt deer in the forest or to take part in one of Murtha's illegal enterprises.

A hunter named Deadeye stood up with a glass of hard cider in his hand. "Fellow feasters," he said, interrupting Beetle's dark thoughts. "Let's raise our glasses to an excellent cook and hunting guide."

The men stood, raised their glasses, and said, "To Murtha."

Halfheartedly participating in the toast, Beetle raised her glass of milk.

Murtha nodded modestly.

The hunters sat down and quickly began passing the masterfully prepared dishes around the table. In spite of herself, Beetle's mood improved as she filled her plate. She was digging her fork into a mound of creamy mashed potatoes when Slugger mentioned a white buck called Splayfoot.

Beetle put down her fork and listened intently.

"He's the biggest albino whitetail in all of Butterball County," Slugger said. "Solid muscle, too. Must go about three hundred pounds."

The stout hunter stood, spread his arms about three feet apart, and said, "His antlers are this wide." Then, apparently satisfied that he'd made his point, he sat back down.

"Why is he called Splayfoot?" Floyd Dooley asked.

"Because his right front foot is slightly turned out to the side," Deadeye said. "His splayed foot and impressive size of his hooves make his tracks easy to identify."

Beetle hadn't noticed if the white buck in the barn had a splayed front foot, but she was convinced he was Splayfoot just the same.

"Deadeye tilted his grizzled chin toward George, Melvin, and Floyd Dooley—the least experienced hunters in the group.

"There is a local legend about an albino buck," he said. "Some folks believe the legend is about Splayfoot. Would you boys like to hear the story?"

The Dooley brothers exchanged glances. After appearing to reach an unspoken consensus they said, "Sure" in unison.

Deadeye rested his elbows on either side of his plate and began. "According to the legend, a magnificent albino buck has roamed this area for hundreds of years. He supposedly acts as a game warden."

"You mean arresting hunters for violating regulations?" George sniggered.

"No. The Albino operates under a different set of rules. He has no problem with hunters who harvest deer lawfully as long as they honor the deer's spirit and thank it for the food that its body provides. But he punishes those who don't."

"What kind of punishment?" Melvin asked, holding a forkful of buttery green beans halfway to his mouth.

Firelight played an eerie shadow show across Deadeye's craggy face. "The Albino lures hunters who deliberately violate his code to a hellish place called Deadman's Swamp, where they're never heard from again."

"If *I* shot a deer, I wouldn't bother honoring its spirit. But I'd gladly thank it for providing me with a big pair of antlers to hang over my garage door," George said, with a smirk.

Deadeye shrugged. "You can scoff at the legend, but the question is: are you willing to accept the consequences if it's true?"

George Dooley turned to his brothers, looking for encouragement. Met by the disgusted expressions on both Floyd and Melvin's faces, his smug smile disappeared.

After hearing George's tactless remarks, Beetle understood why the albino in the legend had no patience with unrepentant hunters. Murtha had said she only provided her services to hunters with high standards. But George's flippant attitude suggested the opposite. In fact, George seemed like the type of hunter who wouldn't think twice about killing a deer turned out for slaughter. The other hunters seemed respectable, though, Beetle thought. But she was prepared to change her mind if their actions should prove otherwise.

Melvin Dooley looked at Murtha. "Do you believe in the legend?"

"No," Murtha said flatly. "There is a simple explanation as to why so many hunters perish in the swamp. They ignore the KEEP OUT DANGER signs clearly posted around its perimeter."

"What makes the swamp so dangerous?" Melvin Dooley asked.

"Quicksand, bottomless pools, confounding fogs that appear out of nowhere, sudden and extreme fluctuations in temperature, maze-like channels. Some even say the swamp is haunted by the ghosts of lost hunters that stalk unwary travelers and drown them."

Just then a log in the fireplace exploded with a spectacular pop. The sharp report echoed off the ceiling, sending a palpable shudder through everyone but Murtha. An uneasy silence lingered in the room until Floyd Dooley said, "Has anyone lost in the swamp ever found a way out?"

"There have been a few, but their minds were permanently damaged by the experience," Murtha said.

"Have you been in the swamp?" Melvin asked Murtha.

"Many times. I know the only safe routes through the swamp. The knowledge has been in my family for generations. I'll be guiding you through a corner of it tomorrow."

Frowns creased the Dooley brothers' faces. They leaned in close and whispered among themselves. Floyd straightened. Meekly raising his hand as if he were back in grade school, he said, "What about a compass?"

Murtha shook her head. "A compass is useless in the swamp. The needle spins around with no rhyme or reason."

The air suddenly went out of the conversation. Sounds of cutlery scraping on plates filled the empty silence.

Beetle was captivated by the possibility that Splayfoot could have had an ancestor that inspired the legend of the Albino. Carrying the thought forward, she wondered if that ancestor's albino descendants could have perpetuated the legend? And if so, might Splayfoot have a male albino offspring in the barn right now? She thought it would be fun to find out.

Eventually, Popshot said, "I've never crossed paths with the Albino, but I've had a few encounters with Splayfoot. He's not easy to find. But if he wants to lead a hunter on a wild chase, he'll leave his super-sized droppings in a prominent place along a well-traveled trail."

"You're right about that. Splayfoot's droppings are his calling card," Deadeye said. "He's the most cunning buck I've ever hunted. What's more, when it's snowy or foggy in the woods, he blends in perfectly."

Slugger nodded. "I remember the first time I lost his trail. The scoundrel came up behind me and snorted. I was so startled I nearly shot myself in the foot."

"Wish I had a penny for every time that red-eyed devil's given me the slip," Popshot said.

Floyd Dooley turned to Deadeye. "How long have you been hunting Splayfoot?"

Deadeye rubbed his chin. "Hmm . . . . as long as I've been coming to Sooty Wick Inn. Must be ten years now. Which reminds me,

Murtha, when are you going to grace this table with one of your amazing pies?"

Murtha waved off the compliment as she stood up. She pointed to a large, flat-topped piece of furniture behind her and said, "Beetle, please take the dessert dishes off the sideboard and put them on the table."

Beetle complied.

The men passed their dinner plates. By the time the plates reached Murtha at the head of the table, they were stacked in a single pile. Murtha carried them to the kitchen, then returned with an apple pie the size of a manhole cover. Each hunter received a generous helping. Blissful smiles spread across the hunters' faces after the men had taken a few bites.

Beetle's pie remained untouched. Nothing she had seen or heard during the meal had lessened her suspicions about Murtha. She definitely needed to continue her investigation. Then if she discovered that the deer were in danger, she would try to reach her parents on their satellite phone in the rain forest and ask them what she should do. And if she couldn't contact them, she would have to stop Murtha on her own.

Somehow.

Moonlight Surprise

The mattress jounced. Beetle woke with a start after glimpsing movement out of the corner of her eye. An odd chattering sound drew her attention. She rolled to her side and saw Jezebel on the windowsill. The cat strained against the glass.

Beetle stumbled to the window and peered out blearily. Silvered by the full moon, the backyard looked almost as bright as day. She expected to see an opossum or a raccoon skulking across the frosted ground. But it was eerily empty. Frowning with concentration, she scanned the yard once more. Again, nothing moved except trees shivering in the wind.

She shifted her gaze upward to the barn roof. Though she knew it was impossible, she thought she saw the metal raven on the weather vane tilt its head toward the ground as if something had suddenly caught its eye. She felt an irresistible urge to follow its gaze.

Her breath quickened. An apparition loosely wrapped in a winding sheet stepped out from behind the barn.

Desperately hoping the ghostly image was a trick of the moonlight, she leaned closer to the window and strained for a better look. All at once the wind died. The winding sheet went limp, giving Beetle a clear view of the figure. It was Murtha in a long white nightgown.

A deep, rumbling purr erupted from Jezebel's throat as if she'd been expecting her mistress to appear all along. Beetle wondered what Murtha was doing out so late.

Moments later, a white buck crossed the moonlit field behind the goat barn and strode up the slope toward the back of the barn. His approach set Beetle's heart pounding. The herd of deer came next, cautiously following in his wake.

She was amazed by what happened next. The buck stood aside, and Murtha stroked each doe and fawn as it entered the barn. When the last deer passed through the door, the white buck bounded back down the slope, crossed the field, and slipped back into the forest of tall pines.

After seeing Murtha pet each deer, Beetle realized the woman meant no harm. She felt a mixture of guilt, embarrassment, and relief. What's more, she was glad to see that Murtha did not hold the deer captive.

Beetle glanced at the alarm clock on the bedside table. The glowing numerals showed 4:30 AM. She assumed Murtha had freed the deer sometime after dark and then gone out to let them into the barn before dawn. A nightly ritual, perhaps? But to what purpose? And then it occurred to Beetle that Murtha was protecting the deer from hunters. An unconventional practice for a hunting guide, but it made her feel a whole lot better about the woman.

Jezebel jumped down from the windowsill and distracted Beetle for an instant. When Beetle looked out the window again, Murtha emerged around the side of the barn and headed toward the inn.

Beetle got back into bed just before Murtha entered the kitchen. Jezebel nudged the bedroom door open and left the room as Murtha's footsteps faded in the direction of the hall.

Dead Man's Swamp

There was a pink glow on the horizon as Murtha parked the VW bus on the roadside. They all got out. Their exhalations instantly turned to steam in the cold dawn air. Deadeye, Popshot, and Slugger headed off one-by-one to their old familiar stands. The Dooley brothers followed Murtha and Beetle into the forest.

Murtha had given Beetle an orange wool cap and one of her own hunting vests to wear over her parka. It had a small, round compass pinned to the pocket.

The long, bulky garment bunched between her knees, nearly tripping her as she struggled to keep up with Murtha's long strides.

The hunting party followed a deeply furrowed game trail edged by soft-needled pine saplings. Early morning light filtered down through a canopy of tall evergreens. An owl glided overhead on muffled velvet wings and vanished between the hemlock trees.

Beetle, George, and Floyd paused on the edge of Deadman's Swamp while Murtha led Melvin to his stand: a crude structure made of long branches propped against a low-hanging limb.

Rejoining the group a few minutes later, Murtha motioned to Floyd and George. "Walk ahead of me," she said. "I'll guide you from behind."

Then turning to Beetle, she admonished, "Rule number one: stay by my side. The swamp is a tricky place. *Never* assume the ice on the pools is thick enough to support your weight. The pools may look shallow, but some of them are deep enough to swallow a house. Rule number two: if you should fail to obey rule number one and we become separated, *stay put*. Blow the whistle I gave you, and I'll come and find you."

Beetle hadn't considered the possibility of getting lost. The thought of being all alone in the swamp raised goose flesh on her arms. Without Murtha's guidance, she could easily drown, step in quicksand, or blunder into a maze.

The hunting party stepped over exposed tree roots and scattered stones along a narrow earthen causeway. Beetle thought it resembled the knobbed ridge of a dinosaur's back. The swamp did not seem menacing as she walked beside Murtha. In fact, she found it strangely beautiful as they ventured deeper into the wetland of downed trees, hummocks of matted grass, and frozen pools.

A column of mist hovering above a depression in the ground suddenly caught Beetle's attention. It looked like the nearest thing to a soul that she could imagine. She watched, mesmerized, as hundreds and then thousands of the shimmering columns ascended from unseen cracks and crevices.

When Beetle finally snapped out of her thrall, she was alarmed to find herself enveloped by a thick, sulfurous-smelling fog. Worse yet, there was no sign of Murtha and the hunting party. Beneath her wool cap, her headband felt too tight, a sign of her growing anxiety.

A rush of panic sent her sprinting blindly down the causeway. She caught her foot on a root and sprawled forward onto the ground. Shaken but uninjured, she scrambled back to her feet, reached for the whistle on a rawhide cord around her neck, pressed it to her lips, and blew. Instead of emitting the piercing sound she had expected, the whistle mewed like a newborn kitten.

She tried several more times, experiencing the same puny results. Finally, assuming the whistle was defective, she slipped it over her head and impulsively cast it aside. Next, she yelled for help. Her voice came out in a faint whisper. Attempting to amplify the sound, she cupped a hand on either side of her mouth and shouted. It made no difference. She was wasting her breath. No one would hear her calls as long as the evil-smelling fog persisted.

Isolated from everything she held familiar, Beetle had never felt more alone. Despite Murtha's warning, she had foolishly allowed herself to be distracted. What good would she be to her parents on a rescue mission if she couldn't follow a simple instruction? Telling herself that Murtha would probably show up at any moment, she tried not to think about all the dangers in the swamp. It was not long, however, before her dark thoughts took over again.

Beetle looked inward. She tried to still her mind. After several minutes, she remembered Murtha had said the hunting party would be traveling in a westerly direction. She looked up at the ceiling of fog. There was no hint of the sun. Without it, she had no hope of finding which way was west. Then it occurred to her that moss was supposed to grow on the north side of trees. But the trees were no more than flat shadows.

Then she reluctantly grasped the small, round compass pinned to her vest and steadied it with her hand. Just as Murtha had said, the needle quivered and lurched wildly on its stem. She released the compass, letting her hand fall limply to her side. Time seemed suspended in the interminable gloom. She began to see shadowy forms that resembled imps and hump-backed trolls skulking among the surrounding bushes. Though the sight unnerved her, she told herself the figures were only an illusion. She peered harder. They were gone.

A second later, she thought she sensed something malevolent reaching out to tap her shoulder. She dared not look behind her, but the prickly sensation became too strong to ignore. She crooked her head around, and was relieved to see swirling tendrils of fog instead of the ghost of a lost hunter.

She brought her hand to her chest to calm her pounding heart and told herself it was a trick of the fog.

Still, the evil presence had seemed too real to be a figment of her imagination. Beetle hugged herself against the cold. She couldn't stand around waiting for Murtha much longer.

Again her skin prickled. This time the sensation went right to her core. She had no doubt that the presence was real. She wanted to run—get away from the thing watching her—but the fog had narrowed her sight to only a foot or so.

Desperate to move, she got on her knees, unzipped her vest so that it would not get in the way, and began to crawl. Feeling her way, she strained her eyes, watching for any trees on the causeway. Although she hadn't seen many, she worried she might not notice one in time to avoid cracking her head on it. Her knees and shins struck stones and exposed roots. Anxious to leave the eerie presence behind, she grimly endured the pain.

She eventually came to a fork in the causeway, but she dared not stray from her present path. A little farther on, the causeway ended abruptly. Another foot and she would have toppled headfirst into what seemed to be a channel of open water. Shaken, she took a steadying breath, slowly blew it out, then reversed direction on her hands and knees.

Beetle found her way back to the fork and took the other way. That path ended several minutes later. Another dead end. She paused and sat back on her heels, resting her battered hands and knees. Everything was unnervingly still. With her soiled mitten she wiped beaded moisture from her face, then squinted at the indistinct landscape.

As best she could tell, dense bushes rooted in interconnecting pools surrounded the causeway. She assumed the hunting party had to have come this way. Yet there was no indication of where they might have gone next.

Beetle had no idea how to proceed. The indifferent fog seemed to mock her. Should she turn back and try to find Melvin on the edge of the swamp? Or continue her search for the hunting party?

Beetle shivered, sensing a sharp drop in temperature. The fog froze instantly, forming tiny ice particles in the air, glazing the surfaces of everything around her. The word *pogonip* popped into her head, another term for ice fog she had learned from her parents. She had found the word amusing back then, but it held no humor for her now.

The causeway was too slippery for her to go back and try to find Melvin. She doubted that leaving the causeway and leaping from bush to bush would be much safer, but she decided to take a chance. She felt that prickly sensation again.

Then something grabbed her arm. Fog stole her scream as she jerked her arm free of a bony hand with long, green fingernails. It resembled something between a plant and an animal. The thing stood maybe ten feet tall, covered from head to toe with long strands of grayish green vegetation. It stank like rotten cabbage.

Beetle scrambled to her feet, and dodging the creature's second attempt to grab her, she hurtled off the causeway. She crashed into the nearest bush, grasping at ice-glazed branches to steady herself. Terrified the thing could be right behind her, she blundered on, leaping from bush to bush over partially frozen water. Her ragged breathing billowed into clouds that instantly merged with frozen fog.

She shifted direction constantly to avoid ice-covered pools too wide to jump. Eventually she paused to look around. A tear of frustration trickled from her eye and stung a welt on her cheek where a branch had lashed her face.

She hadn't wanted to admit it, but she could not deny the truth any longer. She was hopelessly lost and an easy target for the swamp creature.

Then Beetle heard what sounded like ice shattering under foot. Startled, she froze and listened. She peered into dead-still gloom.

She thought she saw a bush quake. It could have been shifting fog. But she had to know for sure.

Again, Beetle strained to see.

The same bush quaked again. This time she knew the movement was real. The bush was maybe five feet away, and it appeared to have a ragged outline unlike the bare bushes surrounding it. Beetle was suddenly hopeful that Murtha had jostled the bush. She had to get Murtha's attention, even if it meant giving away her location to the swamp creature. Praying her voice would carry through the fog, she shouted, "Murtha, I'm here! Over here!"

Beetle jumped to the closest bush. She barely touched down before jumping to the next one. Then she aimed for the ragged bush.

something between a plant and an animal

It was the longest jump she had made. She landed on her knees. Sharp twigs and stiff, leathery leaves dug into her face. She heard more ice breaking, but it sounded fainter than before. Adrenaline pounded through her body. She pulled herself up, scrambled around the bush's narrow base, and shouted, "Wait! Don't leave!"

Her heart felt like a stone. She looked down at the ice in front of her. It was still intact. Murtha would have left a trail of shattered ice if she had come this way.

Beetle held back tears. Crying was a luxury she couldn't afford with the swamp creature possibly lurking nearby. She looked around warily and listened. After several long minutes, she neither heard nor sensed its presence. Just the same, she kept up her guard. All at once, the fog thinned, revealing an open expanse of frozen pools punctuated with hummocks of matted grass, withered ferns, and rotten tree stumps. Surveying the desolate landscape, Beetle held little hope of finding Murtha now.

Murtha had said that people lost in the swamp rarely found their way out. And even if they did, their brains were permanently scrambled by the ordeal. If by some miracle Beetle got out of the swamp on her own, she hoped her mind would still be intact. She felt her face tighten into a grimace. Her tears threatened to fall in earnest.

Then, as all seemed lost, she spotted fresh, exceptionally large deer tracks. Some of the prints turned out to the side. Splayfoot was the only deer she knew of with hoofs fitting that description.

Studying the ground beyond the patch of trampled grass, she could see Splayfoot's tracks leading away from her. Hopeful they would guide her out of the swamp, she decided to follow them. The fog thickened again, shortly settling about a yard above the ground.

Beetle looked nervously behind her. There was no sign of the swamp thing among the bushes. She quickly moved on, following the buck's trail around frozen pools and tree stumps. Eventually she came to a massive beaver dam.

.The buck had crossed the top of the dam, leaving his hoof prints in the smelly, black muck packed between gnawed sticks and branches. Beetle picked up a long, sturdy stick stripped of its bark by a beaver, took a deep breath, and stepped onto the structure.

Water licked at her heels. She tensed as glazed sticks shifted beneath her feet. More than once, she almost pitched off the back of the dam to the frozen marsh below. By the time she reached the other side, Splayfoot's tracks had vanished. Frantic to pick up the trail again, she clutched the beaver stick, and heedless of the potential danger within their depths, scrambled helter-skelter over ice-covered pools.

After a while, she spotted Splayfoot's hoof prints. They were fainter and farther apart than those she had followed previously. Even so, she managed to stay on his trail. Eventually she came to a causeway. Beetle could just make out Splayfoot's tracks on the glazed surface. She moved along slowly, relying on the beaver stick to steady herself. In the distance, she could see flashes of orange through rents in the fog. It must be the hunting party! Beetle impulsively tossed the stick aside and broke into a run.

After several reckless strides, she tumbled off the causeway and crashed through thin ice on a pool. Her heart pounded as she sank into frigid water. She thought her wet clothing was the reason for her rapid decent, but she quickly sensed a swirling current sucking her down. She flailed her arms with all her might as she struggled to keep her head above water.

All at once, a deadening sensation invaded her mind and weakened her will to fight the churning vortex. Her arms and legs grew heavy and unresponsive. Helpless to resist any longer, she slipped beneath the surface. Shocked by the pain of chill water rushing up her nose, she thrashed choking and gasping back to the surface.

She paddled and kicked furiously against the unrelenting current.

Finally, she wrenched her legs free and threw her arms around a rotten tree stump at the edge of the pool.

The current again tried to suck her down, but she found the strength to haul herself out of the pool and crawl back onto the causeway. She lay on her side, exhausted and shivering. Through half-closed eyes, she saw a grayish green form detach itself from the fog. Her eyes shot open with recognition. The swamp creature, and it was coming toward her with alarming speed.

Gasping, she staggered to her feet. Refusing to let her heavy, waterlogged clothing slow her down, she dashed along the causeway. Immediately she noticed no more ice on the ground. The fog had dissipated too. Had she crossed some kind of demarcation line? Beetle had seen it rain on one side of a street and not the other. Maybe the same freaky effect applied here.

She glanced over her shoulder to see if the thing was gaining on her. The causeway was empty. She nearly fell over with relief.

When she finally caught up with Murtha and George and Floyd Dooley, Beetle was overjoyed. She thought they would be happy to see her, too. But her sudden appearance evoked no response from the group. In fact, they didn't seem to realize that she had been missing. Her wide smile drooped into a frown. Were they intentionally ignoring her as punishment for getting lost?

Then she spotted her discarded whistle on the ground. Baffled, she stopped to pick it up. It defied logic to find it within feet of where she had lost track of the hunting party. She tried to hold back panic as she tucked the whistle into her vest pocket.

Though her brain was awhirl with confusion, at least she was certain of her ordeal in the swamp. She glanced down at her clothes and gasped. They were bone dry and free of mud stains.

She stripped off a mitten and felt for the welt on her left cheek. It wasn't there. Her skin was smooth and unblemished. Without any physical evidence to prove that her experience had been real, Beetle didn't know what to think. Maybe the sulfurous-smelling fog had altered her perception. Maybe being lost in the swamp had been an illusion. So why did the hunting party seem unaffected by the fumes? It occurred to her that the adults may not have been susceptible to the tainted vapors because they were bigger than she was.

The possibility that the fog induced her ordeal made sense except that that conclusion didn't explain how the whistle had ended up on the ground instead of around her neck.

The more she tried to find an explanation for the mounting inconsistencies, the more befuddled she became. In fact, she thought she could be losing her mind. It suddenly occurred to her that she was falling behind the hunting party again. She caught up in a hurry, then fell in step beside Murtha.

The sun shone brightly when the group reached firm ground. Beetle looked back at the swamp and shuddered. Her mind was in too much of a tangle to speak of her frightening experiences. Despite her confusion, however, she was certain of one thing—under no circumstances would she stray from Murtha's side on the return trip through the swamp.

Murtha, Beetle, and the two Dooley brothers hiked up a steep, winding trail. A granite ledge rose abruptly to their right. A valley of ancient oaks dropped off to their left. The hunting party took a sharp bend, up another incline, then split off from the trail. After trudging a short distance through scrub brush, they came out onto the granite ledge that Beetle had seen from the trail below.

Murtha turned to Floyd Dooley. "This stand will give you a good view of any deer moving through the oak forest." She gestured to a nearby rock about the size and shape of a hassock. "Set yourself down here if you like." Then she suggested he cut some evergreen boughs to pad the rock's surface to make it more comfortable to sit on. Finally, she told Floyd she would be back before dark.

George Dooley, Beetle, and Murtha returned to the main trail. The climb grew even steeper and the footing more difficult as they dodged washed-out gullies strewn with loose stones and gravel. When they reached the top of Huckle Ridge, Murtha led them to a massive lichen-encrusted boulder situated in the middle of a clearing. "This is your stand, George," Murtha said. She showed him a long cleft in the boulder where he could conceal himself and watch for deer entering the clearing from several directions.

Then Murtha and Beetle returned to the trail and descended the ridge together.

The Journal

Feeling the after effects of lunch and the morning's walk, Beetle felt a gentle weariness creep through her limbs. She went to her room and snuggled next to Jezebel, asleep on the bed.

She awoke about thirty minutes later. The house felt empty. A sharp *thwack* resonated through the inn's walls. She got up and looked out the bedroom window. Murtha was in the backyard chopping wood.

Beetle left the inn. She walked past the two-story ell into the backyard. Straight ahead at the bottom of a long slope, she saw a red barn with the dairy goats penned out front. A field stretched behind the barn and beyond that a forest of tall, dark pines.

Murtha was at Beetle's right, wielding an ax beneath three enormous spruce trees towering behind the inn. Judging from the quantity of freshly split firewood scattered around the base of the chopping block, she had been chopping wood for some time. Shivering despite her warm clothing, Beetle wondered how Murtha stood the cold, coatless, with her shirt sleeves rolled up. She was hatless as well, wearing only a tie-dyed brow band.

Treading on a carpet of rust-colored needles strewn with green, cigar-shaped cones, Beetle approached Murtha. As she drew nearer, she noticed one of the brass buttons that attached Murtha's overall straps to the bib seemed to have gone missing. Murtha had substituted a yellow diaper pin in its place. Beetle smiled inwardly, amused by the super-sized pin and its quirky, duckling-shaped clasp.

Setting a chunk of wood on the chopping block, Murtha gestured for Beetle to stand back. Then she hiked the ax over her head and brought it down, easily cleaving the piece of wood in two. Beetle dodged a barrage of wood chips released by the powerful impact. Then she stepped back several feet, anticipating the next volley of chips.

Murtha chopped wood with a fluid motion that Beetle found mesmerizing along with the satisfying *thwack* the ax made each time it sheared a chunk of wood in two. Lines creased the outer corners of Murtha's eyes, and her long blonde braid was laced with gray. Beetle guessed Murtha was older than her own parents. But beyond that she had no idea of the woman's age.

Murtha put the ax aside. She picked up a hatchet and began chopping the firewood into kindling. By the time she finished, clouds had crowded out the sun.

"I could use some help carrying the kindling inside," Murtha said, waving Beetle forward.

After loading Beetle's outstretched arms, Murtha said, "Put the kindling in the wood bin by the stove. I'll get an armload myself and be right in."

Beetle entered the dooryard just as a shaft of light burst through the clouds, gilding the weather-beaten clapboards on both the ell and the gabled end of the inn.

Her eyes went wide as the inn's shabby facade suddenly appeared grand and inviting. The striking illusion lasted only seconds before the clouds again eclipsed the sun, but it had been long enough to give Beetle a sense of how the inn might have looked long ago. Captivated by the fleeting spectacle, she hugged the bundle of kindling to her chest.

Murtha came up behind Beetle and ushered her into the inn's kitchen. Murtha rekindled the fire in the cook stove and kneaded bread dough on the kitchen counter. Beetle sat down at the kitchen table and opened her journal. She tried to decide which of the day's events to record. She had no interest in writing about her frightening experiences in the swamp. However, the dramatic play of light on the inn she had witnessed about a half hour before seemed like a good choice until a more appealing idea came to mind.

The afternoon passed quickly as the mouthwatering aroma of baking bread filled the kitchen. Beetle was finishing her entry when she felt a tremor pass through the back of her chair. She twisted around in her seat, shocked to find Murtha gazing down at her journal.

Beetle frowned. *How dare Murtha violate her privacy!* Her annoyance quickly turned to embarrassment. She hadn't felt so self-conscious since the beginning of the school year when she accidentally tracked dog poop into homeroom on the sole of her shoe. Now, she wanted to melt under the table, but her gaze remained fixed on Murtha's face.

Murtha blinked as if suddenly waking from a spell. An odd expression flickered across her face. "Sorry," she said. "I didn't mean to read your journal." She turned abruptly and looked out the window above the kitchen counter.

Beetle noticed Murtha's shoulders shaking. After a long minute passed, the woman turned around. Beetle thought she saw her wipe away a tear.

Avoiding Beetle's questioning gaze, Murtha said, "Sun's getting low. The men will wonder what's keeping me." Then she strode into the hall, grabbed her coat and hat, and bolted out the kitchen door.

Murtha was obviously upset. Beetle chided herself for lacking the foresight to work on her journal somewhere other than the kitchen. Looking for something that could have offended the woman, she anxiously read the caption she'd written above her drawing of Murtha.

> *Dec. 2*
>
> *Watching Murtha split firewood this afternoon was quite an experience. I had to clench my teeth to keep my jaw from dropping open. Wham! Her ax came down with the force of a guillotine as she chopped each chunk of wood. The impact made the ground tremble as if the earth's crust were shifting beneath my feet.*
>
> *Move over, Paul Bunyan!*

Beetle shrugged. She may have exaggerated the truth a tiny bit, but as far as she could tell, the caption reflected her admiration for Murtha. Then she considered her drawing. She smiled, approving of the way she had portrayed Murtha's solid stance, the ax raised purposefully above her head. Then she narrowed her eyes and leaned in for a closer look.

finishing a journal entry

She noticed that she could have made the chunk of wood on the chopping block larger. The mistake was a bit disappointing, but it was nothing compared to what she observed next. The too-small chunk of wood blended seamlessly with the chopping block, as if she had done it on purpose, creating the illusion of a person kneeling in front of an executioner.

Shaken, she gaped at the picture. Even without wearing an executioner's hood, Murtha looked as though she was about to lop off the head of a condemned prisoner. She had a sinking feeling that Murtha had seen it too. Even worse, it didn't help matters that she had likened Murtha's ax to a guillotine in the caption.

A lump formed in her throat. Now she had an idea how Dr. Frankenstein must have felt toward his monster. Beetle's shoulders sagged, her eyes downcast. Despite her best intentions she too had created an abomination.

Tender Ego

"How is your ankle?" Murtha asked during lunch the following afternoon.

"Better. Thank you," Beetle said.

Earlier that morning, she had twisted it while walking in the woods with Murtha and the Dooley brothers. At the time, she'd been too preoccupied with Murtha's reaction to her journal to notice where she was going. When they returned to the inn, Murtha had applied an ice pack to Beetle's ankle and then wrapped it in a stretchy, cloth bandage.

With lunch almost over, Beetle finally had the courage to apologize. She hurriedly blurted, "I didn't mean to offend you with my journal entry."

Murtha wrinkled her brow. "What gave you that idea?"

"The way you left in a hurry after you read it."

"Your entry didn't hurt my feelings." Murtha chuckled. "I thought it was a hoot."

Beetle didn't know whether to take Murtha's comment as a compliment or an insult. Her tender ego in the balance, she asked, "Does 'hoot' mean . . . silly?"

"Not at all," Murtha said. "It's my way of saying your entry made me feel great. I almost blushed when I read the flattering things you wrote about me."

Murtha's positive response seemed to suggest that she hadn't seen the unintended illusion in the drawing. But just to be sure, Beetle dared ask, "Did you like the drawing, too?"

Murtha leaned forward and crossed her muscled forearms on the tabletop. "Wonderful," she gushed. "It said more about me than a photograph ever could."

Unaccustomed to such high praise, Beetle got a feathery feeling inside.

"Is there anything else on your mind?" Murtha asked.

Beetle shook her head.

"Good. Now I'd like to get something off my chest. I had no right to read your journal. It's just that once your entry caught my attention—"

"It wasn't your fault," Beetle interrupted. "I practically invited you to read it. Besides, I probably would have done the same thing in your place." Her spontaneous admission came as a revelation to her. She suddenly sat taller in her chair, aware that she and Murtha were not so different after all.

"I'm glad we talked," Murtha said.

Beetle nodded. "Me, too."

Murtha pushed back her chair and stood. "I've got chores to do in the goat barn. Would you like to come along?"

"Sure," Beetle said.

Murtha and Jezebel descended the long slope to the goat barn. Beetle followed several yards behind. Slowed by her sore ankle, she leaned on a furled umbrella for support. Farther on, at the bottom of the incline, she passed a stooped apple tree with a crook in its trunk. It reminded her of an old man with an arthritic hip. A hundred feet or so beyond the tree, she thumped across a wooden footbridge that spanned a dry stream bed.

Murtha entered the goat yard with Jezebel and quickly closed the gate behind her. Beetle caught up a few minutes later. She paused to observe a brightly colored whirligig creaking in the wind.

When Beetle stepped into the yard, Murtha said, "Make sure you shut the gate."

Beetle had no sooner closed it than a big black-and-white goat barreled toward her, scattering a group of does in his wake. He skidded to a halt in front of her and boldly rubbed his horned brow against her arm. In spite of her unease, she petted the shaggy goat with a mittened hand.

After stroking him, she noticed a powerful odor emanating from her mitten. Scrunching her nose, she said, "*What is that stink?* It's ten times worse than the winning entry in a smelly sneaker contest."

Murtha opened the barn door. She chuckled and shook her head. "I've never heard Billy's musk described in quite those terms before. Believe it or not, the does find it irresistible."

"Really?" Beetle scowled at her mitten. She doubted anything could remove the stink short of burning it in the cook stove.

Murtha held Billy back as the does entered the barn. Beetle and Jezebel walked inside next. Murtha followed, quickly shutting the door behind them. "Billy isn't allowed in the barn," she said. "His musk taints the flavor of the does' milk."

With her sinuses still tingly from Billy's sharp scent, Beetle nodded her understanding. She stood beside Murtha and watched the does jog down the center aisle, then enter a large pen at the end of the barn.

Murtha stepped to the right and opened a door. "This is the creamery where I make goat cheese," she said.

Beetle peeked inside the small room, furnished with a stainless-steel counter, sink, and refrigerator along with some equipment she did not recognize.

Murtha and Beetle walked down the aisle together and stopped at the does' pen. Murtha stepped inside and closed the gate. After singling out a white doe, she said, "Beetle, will you get the gate, please?"

Beetle opened the gate and let Murtha and the goat out.

"Will you close the gate behind me?" Murtha asked. "I want the rest of the does penned in for now."

Opening and closing gates was becoming tiresome, Beetle thought. But when the does surged forward and she'd barely managed to keep them from escaping that she understood the importance of securing gates.

Murtha led the white doe to a low wooden bench with an upright frame on one end. The doe hopped up on it and stuck her head through the frame. A small copper bell on her collar jingled with the motion. Then Murtha slid a rod down through the top of the vertical enclosure that reduced the opening to the width of the doe's neck.

The doe immediately began munching grain on the small shelf in front of her.

"Have you ever milked a goat?" Murtha asked.

Beetle wrinkled her brow and shook her head. "No."

"I'll show you how it's done," Murtha said. "Then you can practice on Tildy here."

Before Beetle could refuse, Murtha placed a milk pail on the bench beneath the doe, pulled up a stool, and lowered herself onto it.

Murtha reached under the goat's belly. There were two teats jutting from the udder. Selecting the closest one, she began the demonstration. "Wrap your thumb and forefinger firmly around the base of the teat to trap the milk inside."

Beetle leaned in for a closer look.

"Then close your hand and squeeze the milk out with the rest of your fingers," Murtha continued.

Beetle's eyes went wide as a stream of milk shot out of the teat and drummed the bottom of the pail.

"After the milk is expelled," Murtha said, "loosen your grip to let the teat fill again. That's all there is to it." Murtha repeated the procedure several more times, then looked over her shoulder at Beetle. "Do you have any questions?"

"Should I milk one teat at a time?" Beetle asked.

"Try using a two-handed method. Alternate between the teats," Murtha advised.

Rising from the stool, Murtha said, "Tildy's milk has nearly dried up. You might get a pint or so. When you're done, pour it into Jezebel's bowl." Murtha gestured with her hand. "It's over by the storage cabinet. I have chores to do, but I'll be back in a while."

Beetle sat down on the stool. She gingerly peeled off the smelly mitten and wrapped it inside its mate, then tucked them in her coat pocket. Murtha made milking the doe seem effortless. But Beetle had a feeling it was more difficult than it looked. Still, gathering her nerve, she scooted forward on the stool and timidly stroked Tildy's side. The doe stopped eating and glared at Beetle out the corner of her eye. Sensing the doe's distrust, she nervously reached beneath the goat's udder and gently grasped both teats.

Just then, Jezebel butted Beetle's elbow. Given a start, she tightened her grip on the teats, then quickly released them as the doe jolted backward on the stand. "Tildy, I'm sorry," she said, hoping to appease the agitated doe.

Tildy slanted a withering look at Jezebel and raised a hind leg. Heeding the warning, Jezebel flattened her ears and slinked away. Beetle waited for Tildy to calm down. Then she carefully grasped both teats and squeezed one and then the other. Neither of them released any milk. It took a moment for her to realize that she had relaxed her grip and the milk had flowed back up into the udder.

After practicing for a while, her dexterity improved, but she still hadn't managed to extract a drop of milk. Repeating the procedure once more, Beetle felt sorry for the discomfort she was causing Tildy.

But then, the right teat expelled a solid stream of milk. Beetle was pleased until it missed the pail, splattered the front of her parka, and dribbled down into her lap. Beetle squirmed uncomfortably as the warm liquid soaked through her jeans. She rolled her stiff shoulders, then squeezed the left teat, releasing a jet of milk that shot between her knees and whitened the toes of her boots. Tildy lunged forward suddenly, clipping the pail with a back hoof. Beetle worried that the doe might lash out at her next. To make matters worse, her nose itched. She exhaled sharply, directing a rush of air toward the tip of her nose. The maddening tickle persisted. Without removing her hands from Tildy, she ground her sweaty face into her coat sleeve and finally found sweet relief.

Daring one last attempt, Beetle flexed her cramped fingers and gently gripped both teats. Then she adjusted her wrists—determined

milking Tildy

to get her aim right this time — and squeezed. She whooped as a jet of milk drummed the bottom of the pail, quickly followed by another. As milk continued to flow, Tildy relaxed.

Beetle's headband had migrated to the back of her neck by the time she squeezed the last drop of milk into the pail. She brushed back her sweaty forelock, then slid her headband back in place. Delighted with her accomplishment, she proudly filled Jezebel's bowl. As she straightened, Murtha clapped a hand on her shoulder and said, "Good job. Now you know where the milk you've been drinking with your meals comes from."

Rebelling against the distressing disclosure, Beetle's stomach clenched. Goat's milk was fine for making cheese, but drinking it was an entirely different matter.

"You're kidding about the milk, right?" she asked.

Murtha shook her head and smiled. "It's good to try new things. I doubt you would have drunk the milk if I had told you where it came from beforehand."

Beetle wanted to tell Murtha off for presuming what was best for her. Fighting the impulse to retch, she took deep breaths. Moments later, her queasiness subsided along with her indignation as it occurred to her that Murtha was right. Drinking goat's milk hadn't done her any harm, and she wouldn't have known she was capable of milking Tildy if Murtha hadn't pushed her into it.

Drawn by loud lapping sounds, Beetle and Murtha turned toward Jezebel. Oblivious to the long chain of bubbles dangling from her chin, the cat greedily drank milk from her bowl. Beetle snorted at the comical sight. Murtha seemed to think it was funny, too. They broke into fits of laughter. Murtha leaned against a post to remain upright. Beetle doubled over, clutching her sides and found it hard to catch her breath.

Regaining her composure first, Murtha wiped tears from her pale lashes. "I still have chores to do. Why don't you go back to the inn and have a blueberry muffin? They're in a pastry box on the kitchen counter."

Beetle liked the idea of returning to the inn for a snack. Besides, Murtha's blueberry muffins were the best: moist and buttery with lots of juicy blueberries that melted in her mouth. Realizing how much she enjoyed eating them with a cold glass of goat's milk, she smiled as she limped back to the inn alone.

Later that day, Beetle sat cross-legged on the bed she shared with Jezebel and sketched some pictures of the goats in her journal. After a few enjoyable hours, she had made a portrait of Billy, the smelly, black-and-white buck, and a portrait of a doe that resembled Tildy. She felt good afterward, unburdened by the weight of her lie. If Murtha should ask to see the sketches, Beetle would have real pictures to show her.

sketches

Burning the Midnight Oil

Beetle tossed in bed that night, her mind fraught with conflict. She wanted to tell Murtha that she knew about the deer in the barn, but she feared her confession would ruin their budding friendship. Finally kicking off the rumpled covers, she set out to find Jezebel. Disturbed by all the tossing and turning, the cat had fled the bed earlier. Beetle could smell freshly baked pies cooling on the counter as she walked through the dark kitchen. The tantalizing fragrance of baked apples seasoned with sweet-smelling spices made her instantly hungry for a slice, though she had eaten her fill of Murtha's delicious blueberry muffins that afternoon in addition to a big supper.

The soft glow illuminating the dining room attracted Beetle's attention. She crept toward the room and peeked around the door jamb. Murtha sat at the long dining table and stared down at a paper. The oil lamp on the tabletop cast a golden halo around her head and shoulders while accentuating the worry lines between her brows. Jezebel stood on the table to Murtha's right.

Beetle decided to go back to her room. She felt uncomfortable about spying on the woman. But as she was preparing to leave, Murtha tapped the paper. Sighing heavily, she said, "The situation is grave. Time is running out." She appeared to be talking to Jezebel.

Something on the paper troubled Murtha. Whatever it was, Beetle thought Murtha shouldn't have to shoulder the burden alone. Maybe there was something she could do to help.

Murtha carefully rolled the paper into a cylinder. Then she stood and walked to the bar in the far left corner of the room. She crouched at its base, obscuring Beetle's view. When she straightened and turned around, the paper cylinder was gone.

Beetle watched Murtha return to the dining table and pick up the oil lamp. Itching to find out what was on the paper, Beetle allowed herself a quick glance at the bar, then tiptoed back through the dark kitchen and into her room.

The following morning, Murtha allowed Beetle to stay at the inn to rest her sore ankle. With several hours to herself, she was tempted to look for the paper Murtha had concealed in the bar, but a sudden pang of conscience stopped her. Instead, she decided to use the time to see if Splayfoot had a male albino offspring in the barn.

Her ankle barely pinched when she tested it. She could do without the umbrella cane. Beetle put on her coat and then bundled apple scraps left over from the pies Murtha had made the previous night into a cloth napkin, slipped it into her pocket, and called Jezebel.

They left the inn through the tunnel and entered the barn a short time later.

Jezebel touched noses with the deer and rubbed her cheek against their long, slender legs while Beetle distributed apple scraps among the does and fawns. The white buck was absent. She assumed he was in the forest.

Beetle found the herd's woodsy scent intoxicating. She flicked on the flashlight and cautiously approached the group of youngsters at the back of the barn. When she was within five feet of them, they scampered off and then stopped a short distance away. Sensing they were playing a game of catch-me-if-you-can, she folded her arms across her chest and ignored them. Within minutes, they pressed in around her feet.

There were ten fawns in total, all male, each one sporting a pair of tiny brow buds. None of them displayed Splayfoot's distinctive white hide. Beetle sat down on a hay bale to order her thoughts.

Why were there no female fawns in the barn? Male adolescent deer were absent as well. She wondered if the young bucks were in the forest fending for themselves. If so, she thought it was still possible that Splayfoot could have at least one albino son among them.

It was close to noon—time to leave the barn. She let out a gasp as she headed toward the ramp. The window that she had climbed through three days earlier was open. How had she missed seeing it when she walked past it this morning? Now aware of her careless mistake, she tried to recall how it had happened. With sickening clarity, she could see herself standing outside the window when Jezebel appeared on the windowsill. Having thought Jezebel might try to run away again, she had scooped the cat up in her arms and then hurried back to the inn. Closing the window had completely slipped her mind.

Beetle assumed Murtha hadn't seen the open window or she would have heard about it. She felt terrible just the same. A predator could have gotten inside the barn and attacked the deer because of her blunder.

She rushed over to the window and lowered the sash, determined never to let anything like this ever happen again. Murtha's friendship and the herd's safety meant too much to her.

Painting the Town Brown

"Beetle get your coat," Murtha called from the kitchen that afternoon. "I have errands to run in town."

Beetle was in her bedroom reading *The Case of the Missing Casket.* Murtha's call interrupted the story just as Greta Spleen was about to reveal the thief's identity. Beetle reluctantly marked her place in the book and put it down.

Stepping into the kitchen, she was surprised to see Murtha wearing a brown bowler hat with a turkey's tail feather tucked in the band instead of her usual hunting cap.

A wicker hamper filled with rounds of waxed goat cheese sat on the kitchen table. Murtha lowered the lid and fastened the latch. "The cheese is for Swindell's Market," she explained. Then she motioned to cardboard pastry boxes on the counter and said, "The apple pies are going to the Scattershot Café. After the deliveries are done, we'll stop at Ashcraft's Hardware and get grain for the goats."

The VW bus lurched over rutted dirt roads and passed dark spruce forests, brown pasture land, and ghostly beaver swamps. Beetle held her breath as the bus trundled over a narrow wooden bridge, loose planks clattering beneath the tires. Black water swirling below sent a shiver up her spine.

The village green finally came into view. Surrounded by a white rail fence, the long rectangle contained a rusted Civil War cannon, several park benches, and a bandstand with peeling white paint. The bus's engine made a tinny racket that echoed off white two-story houses lining Hickory's main street.

The bus slowed as it passed a green three-story Gothic-style Victorian that featured multiple chimneys and turrets, steeply pitched roofs, and recessed balconies. The large sign out front read PIEDMONT FUNERAL HOME.

Murtha turned into the parking lot next door to the ornate building and parked beside a shiny black hearse. After the engine sputtered to a stop, she said, "Wait here. I'll be right back."

Beetle felt an icy chill. She regarded funeral homes and hearses as harbingers of misfortune. Ignoring them, she watched Murtha carry the boxed pies into the Scattershot Café. A wooden sign hung above the door, riddled with what looked like real bullet holes. She sighed, comparing the dingy-looking coffee shop to the fashionable cafés that she and her sixth-grade classmate Stella Piccolo frequented on Newbury Street in Boston. A battered pickup truck backed into the empty space beside the bus. After coming to a full stop, it neverthe-less remained in motion, jouncing wildly on its wheels. The driver's door opened with an earsplitting metallic screech. Out jumped a scrawny man in a rumpled blue uniform. He shouldered a bulging leather mailbag and dashed to the wooden pen mounted on the back of the truck to remove a cane from the topmost slat.

Beetle held her breath as he thrust the blunt end between two slats, viciously prodding a pair of indistinct creatures, prompting sharp squeals and grunts. Her first impulse was to rush to the animals' defense and wrestle the cane away from the man. But lacking the strength to stop him, she feared he would strike her as well.

The commotion inside the pen abruptly stopped. A twisted grin crossed the man's bony face as he hung up the cane. The action gave Beetle the impression he enjoyed tormenting the defenseless creatures. She narrowed her eyes at him, hoping he would get a taste of his own medicine someday.

He drew closer to the bus and paused to survey the main street. A malicious glint in his eyes suggested he was the gossipy type. Then he spotted Beetle through the window and smirked, as if he was enjoying a private joke. Beetle's eyes went wide when she noticed small white bubbles seeping out the corners of his mouth. When she was six, she had mixed water with a tube of denture cream belonging to her family's housekeeper, Ms. Blister. The results had looked a lot like the foam dribbling down either side of his hatchet-shaped chin. The memory brought a spontaneous smile to her face despite the man's repulsiveness. Her fixed stare seemed to make the man aware of his appearance. He dabbed his lips and examined the froth clinging to his fingertips, then mopped his mouth with his coat sleeve. He gave Beetle a look that could have stopped a train and shook his fist at her. Swallowing her smile, she shrank down in her seat, glad for the barrier of glass and steel between them.

Beetle sagged with relief when the man abruptly turned his back and swaggered off toward the stores. She sat up and shifted her gaze. A small, beady eye peered at her through a gap at the bottom of the pen. With the creature's thick, sausage-like body pressed against the slats, she could see that it was a muddy pig.

Butting the first pig out of the way with its snout, a second muddy pig barged into view. Tempers flared. Once more, the truck jounced to the tune of deafening squeals and grunts. Brown muck flew out of the pen and splattered Beetle's side of the bus just as Murtha stepped out of the café.

Peering out the windshield between clots of pig poop, Beetle watched Murtha approach the pen. The woman said something to the pigs that settled them down. Then she gestured for Beetle to get out of the bus on the driver's side.

Two elderly women in the checkout line at Swindell's Market clucked their tongues and began to whisper as Murtha walked past them. After paying for their groceries, the women stepped aside and continued to whisper until they noticed Beetle's frosty stare. They glared back at her, then hitched up their paper sacks and hurried out of the store as fast as their spindly legs could carry them.

Despite sawdust sprinkled on the black-and-white tile floor, the inside of the market looked immaculate and smelled strongly of disinfectant. A garland of plastic sausage links hung from the ceiling above a glass-fronted counter containing loaves of turkey, salami, bologna, and liverwurst. Beetle's gaze traveled to a vertical glass cabinet where rotisserie-cooked chickens performed endless somersaults beneath the glare of heat lamps.

She sidled over to another counter, this one featuring rows of gutted fish arranged on beds of crushed ice. Sprigs of bright green parsley garnished their slit throats like bow ties. They stared up at her with vacant eyes and bewildered frowns. Sensing the fishes' last desperate moments in the deeps, Beetle recoiled from the counter.

"Don't they look natural?" The voice came from behind her.

Startled, Beetle turned to see a man with dark, hypnotic eyes. He wore a straw boater and red apron over a black tuxedo. She wrinkled her nose, enveloped by a cloud of sickly sweet cologne.

"Marley Swindell, at your service," he said, pressing a white business card into her palm. She looked down at it and read the gold embossed letters.

SWINDELL'S MARKET
Marley Swindell — Purveyor of
Fine Meats, Cheeses, Fish, and Poultry

She automatically flipped it over. The other side read:

PIEDMONT FUNERAL HOME
Marley Swindell — Mortician and Director
"We Lay Out Your Loved Ones in Style"

Struck by the perversity of Marley's dual occupations, she suppressed an urge to shout, "Yuck!"

"I presume you're the little miss staying with Murtha," he said with oily eloquence. As she gazed mutely at Marley, Beetle's brain had seemingly disconnected from her tongue. After a long moment, she said, "Yes, I'm Beetle Beane."

"Glad to meet you, Beetle." Marley put a hand on her shoulder. She glanced at it and observed dense patches of black hair on the backs of his long, pale fingers. He propelled her toward a large wooden barrel. Sharp dill fumes exploded in her sinuses as Marley folded back the barrel's hinged lid. "Have a juicy pickle, on the house," he said.

Through watery eyes, she saw bumpy, green pickles bobbing in dark brine. They reminded her of the bloated bullfrogs preserved in jars of formaldehyde in the science lab at school. Feeling queasy, she stammered, "N-no, thank you."

"Hello, Marley," Murtha said as she rounded a corner.

"I was just offering Beetle one of my famous dill pickles," he said.

Looming large like a guardian angel, Murtha said, "Let's get a move on, Beetle. We have another stop to make."

Marley looked at his watch. "I've got to be going, too. I have a deceased client to prepare at the funeral parlor."

"I'll have another batch of cheese for you soon," Murtha said, hastily nudging Beetle out the door.

"Glad to hear it. It's one of the store's best sellers," Marley called after them.

Out on the sidewalk, the townspeople gave Murtha sidelong glances. Beetle was beginning to think that the people of Hickory were a bunch of ill-mannered bumpkins. Uncertain what to expect next, she warily followed Murtha into the hardware store. A bell jingled as they stepped inside.

Murtha introduced Beetle to Mr. and Mrs. Ashcraft. The couple contrasted sharply in appearance. Elton was tall, thin, and spiffily dressed. Bernice was short, round, and dowdy, wearing a flowered house dress and baggy cardigan sweater.

"Have a look around, Beetle," Murtha said, "while Elton and I get the grain from the storeroom."

Beetle followed a rapid, clickety-clack noise. It led to a display window where a toy train raced along a track that circled a shiny red chainsaw and a wheelbarrow heaped with fifty-pound bags of sunflower seeds.

A large ceiling fan stirred the air, mixing the rank smell of fertilizer with the fruit scent of candles. The walls and warren-like aisles were jammed with a wide variety of goods. Beetle preferred the diffused daylight slanting through the hardware's cluttered interior to the blaring neon lights of Swindell's Market. Soon, she was lost in an amazing hodgepodge of merchandise. Her gaze flitted over kerosene lamps, sunbonnets, horse and pony halters, stainless steel milk pails, and metal tins of Udder Balm.

Bernice scuffed toward Beetle in carpet slippers. Smoothing the front of her house dress, she said, "Can I help you find something, dear?"

Beetle liked the sound of Bernice's high, fluty voice. The woman's wispy gray hair and soft brown eyes, magnified by the round lenses of her old-time glasses, made her look like a grandmotherly mole in a storybook.

"I'm looking for two presents," Beetle confided. "You have so many interesting things; I'd like to look around for some ideas."

"Well, I'll leave you to it, then. If you need help, give me a call," Bernice said.

Beetle quickened her search when she saw Murtha and Elton come out of the storeroom, each carrying a sack of grain. She heard the bell above the door jingle as they exited the store.

A few minutes later, the bell jingled again. Beetle noticed two men dressed in coonskin caps and grubby insulated coveralls enter the store as she stood at the end of an aisle stocked with household cleaning supplies.

A rabbit pelt and sheathed knife hung from each of their belts. Beetle guessed they were fur trappers. The soles of their boots shed clods of mud as they approached a large peanut bin.

The bell jingled once more. This time Elton and Murtha walked down the main aisle on their way back to the storeroom. Apparently particularly interested in Murtha, the two men turned their heads toward her before stuffing their pockets with handfuls of peanuts.

Then they strolled over to a pot-bellied stove at the back of the store where they began a lively conversation while warming their backsides. Shattered husks rained down around their boots as they extracted the peanuts.

Beetle had a feeling the men might be talking about Murtha. She crept closer, hoping to overhear what they were saying. She wrinkled her nose. From ten feet away, she detected a combination of stale sweat and bacon grease emanating from their bodies. Still straining to hear their conversation, she feigned interest in an evil-looking pronged device designed to harpoon unsuspecting moles burrowing underground.

Their mouths filled with peanuts, everything the men said sounded like gibberish. Frustrated, Beetle crept as close as she dared without being seen. Suddenly, Bernice scurried toward the two men. She glanced at Beetle for a split second, then brandished a feather duster and said, *"Skinner and Foxy Boil.* You should be ashamed of yourselves for repeating that rubbish. I'll thank you to take your business elsewhere from now on."

Bernice's ability to understand the Boils' garbled speech amazed Beetle. She stepped out into the open. She saw that Bernice's countenance had changed from kindly grandmother mole to rabid badger and stood frozen, not knowing whether to stay put or take cover behind a stack of boxed camp toilets.

"What's the big deal? The whole town's talking about it," Foxy protested, a wad of chewed peanuts wedged in his cheek.

"Yeah, give us a break," Skinner said, spraying peanut crumbs and spittle into the air. Resembling a pair of gorillas on steroids, the brothers postured as they glared at Bernice. Bernice glared back at them. She pointed to the door and said, *"Scat!* Or I'll take this feather duster to both of your peanut-pilfering hides."

After a long moment, the Boils backed off and then stomped out the main aisle. The bell jingled violently as they slammed the door behind them. Bernice straightened her house dress, gave Beetle a little wave, then headed toward the counter.

Beetle was relieved that the standoff had ended peacefully. Still, as she went back to shopping, she wondered if the Boils' gossip had something to do with Murtha. About ten minutes later, Beetle placed a yellow bandanna and red leather cat collar, studded with rhinestones, on the counter.

"I see you found what you were looking for," Bernice said, back to her kindly self again.

"They're a surprise for Murtha," Beetle offered, beaming.

Bernice nodded her understanding and pressed the keys on the old metal cash register. It made an ominous grinding sound. Half expecting the brass-plated dinosaur to explode, Beetle stepped back. The numbers 17.99, preceded by a $, popped up in a small glass window at the top of register. Then a shrill bell dinged, and the cash draw shot open faster than her eyes could follow. She cautiously approached the counter again. Digging into her jeans pocket, she pulled out the twenty-dollar bill her mom had given her and handed it to Bernice.

"Would you like me to wrap the presents?" Bernice asked while handing Beetle her change. "I don't have fancy paper, but I'm sure I can find something."

Beetle glanced uneasily at the storeroom door.

After following Beetle's gaze, Bernice said, "Don't worry. Murtha's busy gabbing with Elton. There's still time to wrap the presents before she comes to the counter."

"Sure. That would be great," Beetle said.

Gifts in hand, Bernice shuffled into a small cluttered office behind the counter. A short while later, she returned with two packages neatly wrapped in newspaper and bound with garden twine. Beetle was pleased with the way Bernice had done them up and thanked her for it.

Bernice put the gifts in a small paper bag. She looked troubled as she handed it to Beetle. The corners of her mouth turning down, she said, "I'm sorry the Boils spoke about Murtha that way."

Apparently, Bernice assumed Beetle had overheard the Boils' conversation, thus confirming her suspicion that the men had been talking about Murtha. The whispering directed toward Murtha at Swindell's Market and the curious looks on the street suddenly made sense. Now that Bernice had broached the subject, Beetle said, "Should we warn Murtha that people are gossiping about her?"

"No." Bernice shook her head. "I don't want to bother her with idle talk. She has enough on her mind, putting up the hunters and all."

Just then, Murtha approached the counter. She carried a sack of grain. Beetle discreetly slipped the paper bag into her coat pocket. Shy, she planned to leave the presents on the kitchen table just before she went home in a few days.

Bernice put the grain on Murtha's bill and then bid them goodbye.

Avoiding the pig poop, Beetle entered the bus through the driver's side while Murtha stowed the last bag of grain in the back. The truck with penned pigs was still parked beside the bus. Beetle gestured to it when Murtha got into the bus. "I saw the mailman beat his pigs. It was awful."

"His name is Manuel Flush." Murtha frowned and clenched her hands on the steering wheel. "The animal inspector has taken his livestock away more times than I care to remember. Unfortunately, the authorities haven't been able to shut him down permanently."

Beetle scrunched up her face. "Why does he haul pigs in his truck while delivering mail?"

"He buys and sells farm animals on his mail route."

"I doubt the postmaster would approve," Beetle commented.

"His uncle *is* the postmaster," Murtha explained. Backing the bus onto the main street, she glanced over at Beetle. "You and Bernice seemed to get along well together."

"She's nice," Beetle said, appreciative of the way Bernice had come to Murtha's defense and for her reassurance that the gossip circulating around town about Murtha was harmless.

Peaceful in her mind, she rested her head against the back of the seat and enjoyed the ride back to the inn.

Morris McNab

Early the next morning Beetle lay in bed half awake, listening to the hunters' voices in the kitchen. Her stomach growled, aroused by the savory aromas flooding into her room. She heard the rattle of plates as the men helped themselves to the buffet breakfast on the kitchen table. Soon, all sounds of activity faded to the dining room.

A set of headlights streaked across the backyard briefly striping the ceiling of Beetle's room. Jezebel jumped down from the bed, her silhouette backlit by a sliver of light coming through the crack in the door.

Moments later, Beetle heard the latch on the kitchen door lift with its distinctive snap and Murtha say, "Well, if it isn't the game warden. Glad you could drop by, Morris McNab. Come on in."

"Murtha, I'm not here on a social call," an unfamiliar voice replied.

"Is there a problem?" Murtha asked.

"I might as well get to the point. Manuel Flush reported you to my boss at the Department of Fish and Wildlife. He said he saw a deer looking out a window in your barn when he was on his mail route."

Fully awake now, Beetle sat bolt upright and inhaled sharply. That horrible mailman had seen the deer in the barn window because she had left it open! The Boils must have been talking about it in the hardware store the day before. She wondered if everyone thought Murtha provided captive deer to hunters who came to the inn. Beetle guessed that Bernice had dismissed the men's story because she refused to hear anything bad said about Murtha.

"That's a good one!" Murtha chuckled. "Was it stuffed or alive? Flush has quite an imagination, especially when he's had a nip or two."

"Flush is bad news, drunk or sober," the game warden said. "I wouldn't be surprised if he made up the story. Did you do something to make him angry?"

"We've had some disagreements over the way he treats his animals," Murtha said.

"He has ruined people's reputations for less. In any case, seeing as it's against the law to keep a deer in captivity without a permit, I have to search your barn on the state's behalf."

Beetle's heart squeezed in her chest. If it was a crime to keep a single deer in captivity, what kind of punishment would the state exact for an entire herd? In her mind's eye, she envisioned the game warden setting the deer free and then taking Murtha to jail in handcuffs. It was all Beetle's fault. Her carelessness had brought this trouble to Murtha.

She leaped out of bed. Groping in the near-dark room, she found her jeans draped over the back of a chair and pulled them on over her pajama bottoms. Her breath came in shallow gasps as she peeped through the narrow opening in the door. She immediately spotted the game warden. He was dressed in a dark green uniform with an insignia stitched on his jacket.

Jezebel paced back and forth between the bed and the door.

"Have you got time for breakfast, Morris?" Murtha asked, sounding remarkably calm to Beetle despite the impending search. "If there's a deer in my barn, I'm sure it will keep until you're done eating."

McNab checked his watch. "Sure. A couple of minutes won't make much difference."

Murtha picked up a plate and loaded it with enough scrambled eggs, bacon, ham, home fries, and pancakes to feed an army before handing it to McNab.

If the game warden managed to consume everything on his plate, Beetle doubted he would feel well enough to search the barn afterward. She suspected that was what Murtha had in mind. It was an inspired plan, and Beetle hoped it would work. However, there was too much at stake for her not to take action on her own, even if it meant breaking the law.

Murtha took a plate for herself and selected a piece of toast and a thin slice of melon. The meager helping was nothing compared to her usual breakfast. Beetle could see that Murtha was more anxious than she let on.

Beetle watched Murtha and the game warden take their plates to the dining room. She wanted to retrieve her coat and boots from the hall, but she couldn't risk being seen.

Moving away from the door, in half-darkness, Beetle located her suitcase on the floor at the foot of the bed. She unzipped it. The noise sounded like an angry bumblebee, amplified. Her hands found a pair of high-top sneakers, an oversized Wonder Woman sweatshirt, and a spare pair of mittens.

Unable to find a pair of socks in the disarray, she abandoned her search, yanked the sweatshirt over her pajama top, and jammed her bare feet into the sneakers. Her fingers were shaky, and it took several tries before she managed to tie the laces.

A quick look at the alarm clock told her it was 5AM. How long before dawn, she wondered. She peeked into the kitchen again. Seeing no one, she opened the door slowly. Jezebel squeezed through the opening and darted into the kitchen.

Beetle crept to the kitchen counter and carefully opened the left-hand drawer. Her heart hammered as she took a flashlight and loaded two batteries into it as quickly as her trembling hands would allow, then closed the drawer. She tiptoed toward the cellar door. Each time a floorboard creaked underfoot, she held her breath, then nervously looked toward the dining room to make sure the noise hadn't attracted attention before she dared move on.

Crossing the kitchen seemed to take an eternity. Finally reaching the cellar door, she impulsively peeked into the front hallway. To her alarm, less than ten feet away, she saw the game warden seated at the table in the dining room. She caught her breath as he looked up in her direction. She ducked behind the door frame.

Any minute she expected him to come through the hall and find her cowering beside the cellar door and then ask who she was and what she was doing up this early in the morning. If her cover was blown, there would be no hope of carrying out her plan.

Beetle swallowed hard and waited. A long time seemed to pass, although it was probably no more than a few minutes. Apparently the game warden hadn't noticed her after all. She cautiously thumbed the latch on the cellar door. It held fast and then lifted with a loud snap that sounded to her like a rifle shot. Had it carried to the dining room? she wondered tensely.

Beetle didn't wait to find out. She opened the cellar door and slipped through the opening with Jezebel. Commanding herself to calm down, she pulled the door shut behind them and slowly eased the latch into its cradle.

Beetle took the flashlight from her sweatshirt. She switched it on just in time to see Jezebel streak down the stairs. Beetle followed as soundlessly as she could. But the worn treads chirped like a chorus of housebound crickets beneath her feet, betraying her progress. She reached the closet and halted. The back of her neck prickled. Was the game warden standing behind her? Barely daring to breath, she glanced over her shoulder and shined the light. No one was there. She wanted to laugh at her foolishness and sob with relief at the same time.

After inhaling several deep breaths, she pulled the closet door open. It let out a harsh bark. She frowned worriedly at the ceiling, certain she was standing directly below the dining room. If she kept making noise at this rate, someone was bound to hear her.

She stepped into the closet with Jezebel at her heels and inched the door shut, producing only a slight squeak. The dark space soothed her jangled nerves as she took a few moments in silence to gather her thoughts. Then she pushed the false panel aside and plunged into the tunnel.

Jezebel took the lead. Beetle sprinted after her. The soles of her sneakers slapped the packed earth and echoed off the tunnel walls. A short distance ahead, two pairs of glowing eyes blinked in the flashlight's beam. She dug in her heels and skidded to a stop within inches of the disembodied orbs. Then she stumbled back, stifling a scream. Jezebel stood dangerously close to a porcupine with its quills fully raised. The prickly rodent gave off a foul odor that nearly caused Beetle to gag. Swallowing her fear of becoming a human pincushion, she inched into a crouch. Her insides quivered as she gathered Jezebel into her arms.

Beetle's trembling legs threatened to give way as she slowly straightened. Taking a much-needed breath, she flattened herself against the wall. The porcupine suddenly whirled around and lashed its barbed tail, nearly harpooning Beetle's foot with its quills. To make matters worse, Jezebel chose that moment to squirm in her arms. After simultaneously restraining the cat and edging unscathed past the porcupine, Beetle discovered her powers of concentration were greater than she thought.

At a safe distance from the porcupine, Beetle put Jezebel down on the ground, and they both took off running. Within moments, she and Jezebel reached the ramp. The encounter with the porcupine had slowed Beetle's progress. Hoping the game warden had barely put a dent in his breakfast, she bit her lip anxiously. A sound similar to a newborn baby's cry pierced the darkness, interrupting her thoughts.

Beetle spun around. Like something out of a nightmare, the porcupine's Troll-Doll face shone in the flashlight's beam. Wailing a second time, the foul-smelling rodent bustled toward her. Beetle turned and bolted to the top of the ramp.

The deer raised their heads when Beetle came around the partition hotly pursued by the bawling porcupine. Just as Beetle was losing all hope of implementing her plan, the porcupine broke off its chase and climbed the ladder to the hayloft. It stepped off the top rung onto a horizontal beam and walked out to the center where it appeared to settle down for a nap.

Beetle sighed, relieved beyond measure. She walked over to the white buck and looked down at his right hoof. It was splayed just as she had expected. She knew Splayfoot possessed a high degree of intelligence, but she wasn't certain how to convey her message. Did he understand English? She tried talking to him first. "The game warden is going to search the barn soon. If he finds you and the rest of the herd here, Murtha will be in a lot of trouble."

Comprehension flashed in his eyes. Then Beetle said, "Do you want to lead the herd out the barn door? Or . . . " with her own plan in mind, ". . . hole up in the inn's cellar with the herd?"

The buck looked past Beetle, appearing to assess the two possibilities. Seconds later, snorting loudly, he assembled the herd. He strode through the opening in the partition. Relieved that the buck trusted her, Beetle kept up with him as they both approached the doorway that led to the ramp. She swept the burlap curtain aside and held it back to let the deer pass.

Splayfoot went down the ramp first, the does and fawns close behind. They gathered in the barn's cellar and waited. Beetle drew the curtain closed behind her and then scooped Jezebel into her arms before hurrying down the ramp herself to join the herd. When she reached them, Splayfoot nodded his head for her to lead his family through the tunnel and into the inn's cellar.

Beetle dashed inside the tunnel. Empowered by the deer's energy at her back, she had never run faster nor felt more exhilarated. At the end of the tunnel, Beetle opened the false panel, eased the closet door open, and released Jezebel. Then she returned through the false panel and held it open for the herd. Her stomach tightened when she saw that Splayfoot's antlers were too broad to fit through the opening in the back of the closet. Meanwhile the herd jammed the passageway. Just as the jostling deer came dangerously close to crushing Beetle, the buck turned his head to one side, slipped his antlers through the opening, and stepped into the closet. He quickly repeated the slick maneuver and entered the cellar.

The herd followed him and settled down quickly. Beetle took a moment to catch her breath. With the deer hidden and safe from discovery by the game warden, the first part of her plan had

no time to hesitate

succeeded. To complete it, she still had to move the goats from their barn to the big barn. She prayed that when the game warden found the goats there, he would then reason that the mailman had seen a goat in the window instead of a deer, the matter would be closed, and Murtha's reputation would be preserved. She estimated it would take no more than ten minutes to make the switch as she hurried back through the tunnel and up to the main floor of the barn.

Beetle gasped, shocked by an unexpected blast of snow as she slid open the barn door. She put on her mittens and pulled up the hood of her sweatshirt. There was no time to hesitate. Leaving the barn door partly open, she turned on the flashlight and plunged into the tempest. She lowered her head against the onslaught of snow streaming down from the still dark sky.

Keeping to shadows just beyond light shining from the kitchen windows, she started down the slope to the small barn where the goats lived. Snow on the ground already piled several inches above her high-top sneakers. After some minutes, she paused and glanced behind her. The inn's lights were no longer in sight.

When the ground leveled, she wiped snow from the flashlight lens and directed a narrow beam in a wide horizontal arch. Cascading flakes mirrored the light and erupted into a blinding curtain of white. To lessen the glare, she lowered the light and then turned in a tight circle. There were no visible landmarks to help her establish her location. A sickening feeling rose in her stomach as she sensed she'd gone off course. Panic threatened to overcome her. Despite wet flakes falling all around, her mouth felt parched. Merciless wind sliced through her cotton sweatshirt and jeans. Hunching her shoulders, Beetle turned and followed her tracks back the way she had come. Long minutes passed before she saw the inn's lights above the crown of the incline. They looked like smeared butter through the falling snow.

She traversed the side of the slope and found its center by aligning herself with the inn. Then she resumed her trek to the goat barn. Her light glanced across a tree. On closer inspection, she saw the crook near its base and recognized it as the old apple tree at the bottom of the slope. If she remembered correctly, it was about a hundred feet from the goat barn.

Eager to reach her destination, Beetle blinked snow from her lashes and dashed forward. She made headway until the ground abruptly fell away. Too late, she realized she had forgotten to consider the ditch running beneath the footbridge before she started off. She landed hard on her side. Her body felt leaden as she lay in a daze. Fat snowflakes spattered her face, but she couldn't will her hand to wipe them away. Then, she heard a wheezy clatter. Slowly she connected the sound with the whirligig outside the goat yard.

Stirring, she sat up with a groan. Her eyes teared up from pain in her left shoulder. Beetle wobbled to her feet, recovered the flashlight, and pointed it in front of her. The beam revealed a number of snow-covered outcrops and whip-thin pine saplings projecting from the embankment. She turned off the light and tucked it into her sweatshirt in order to free both hands.

It took a moment or so to find a firm foothold. She stepped on it with her left foot, then raised her left arm. She fought pain in her shoulder as she groped for a place to hang on. Her mittened hand found a sapling, and she grasped it. A mini-avalanche fell from its branches. Beetle flinched, blinking snow out of her eyes.

She raised her right arm and felt for a handhold. She found another sapling, grabbed it, and turned her head to avoid a fresh volley of snow. Her right foot gained traction next. For a precarious moment, she nearly slid backwards as she transferred her weight from her left foot to her right. From then on, she made slow but steady progress up the embankment.

Standing on flat ground again, she lamented the precious time and energy she had lost. She retrieved the flashlight from her sweatshirt and thumbed the switch. Tired, cold, and aching, she plodded on. Soon her light swept across a section of wire fencing checked with snow. Aided by the whirligig's clatter, she found the gate to the goat yard. Her numb fingers felt as if they might shatter as she clumsily unlatched the gate.

Billy appeared out of the roiling snow as she stepped into the goat yard. His eyes reflected red in the flashlight's beam. Beetle entered the barn with Billy. She intentionally left the door open behind them. Then she raced down the aisle and opened the door to the does' pen. The does swarmed into the aisle and followed Billy out of their barn. Murtha had said the goats would return to the big barn if given the chance. Beetle crossed her fingers, hoping they wouldn't fail her now.

The goats left a wide swath of hoof prints behind that resembled a rumpled rug. Beetle followed their tracks out of the yard and across the footbridge. The long slog uphill was exhausting. As she crested the slope, she thought she saw a figure at the kitchen window. She froze, then realized it had been a low hanging spruce bough swaying in the wind. Her heart still pounding, she trudged on.

The goats' tracks funneled into the barn. Soaked and trembling, Beetle passed through the door. She made an alarming discovery as she moved the light back and forth. Tildy was missing. The realization felt like a punch in the gut!

Missing

A jolt of panic sent Beetle back into the raging storm to find Tildy. She closed the barn door behind her and followed the goats' rapidly disappearing tracks left when they had traveled from their home to the big barn earlier. Wind boomed, bombarding her with snow from all sides as she continued down the slope. Trees limbs splintered and snapped somewhere in the forest.

She gasped as a bucket-size object glanced off her shoulder. Sensing more unseen debris threatening to come within inches of striking her, she defensively hunched her shoulders. Icy pain pricked her fingers and toes. As she took each hard-won step, the slope seemed to grow longer. Beetle could not help thinking that nature was conspiring against her.

Despite the blizzard, Beetle managed to find the old apple tree. She leaned against its snow-pasted trunk to catch her breath, then continued toward the goat barn. A few minutes later, she crossed the footbridge and glimpsed the nearly buried fence ahead.

She searched the yard first, then the inside of the barn. There was no sign of Tildy. Disheartened and weary, she left the barn, trudged across the yard, and slumped against the gate. Her face and ears had long since gone numb. Tears filled her eyes, freezing immediately on her lashes. She had no idea where to look for Tildy next. Finding a white goat in a blinding snowstorm seemed like an impossible task.

Hugging herself against the wind, she set off across the footbridge. Her teeth chattered violently and sent wrenching tremors through her neck and shoulders. Her limbs were beyond freezing now. She couldn't take another step. Her heartbeat even seemed to have slowed down. Still, she knew she had to summon the will to go on, or she and Tildy were liable to freeze to death. Struggling to concentrate, she shut her eyes. An image of her parents flashed in her mind. She was afraid she might not survive to see them again.

Somehow, she found a tiny drop of strength. She felt her pulse quicken. Enlivening muscles and limbs, warmth glowed inside her chest and slowly spread throughout her body. Her skin tingled with life. The weight of exhaustion lifted from her lungs, and she took a deep restorative breath. Her energy and resolve renewed, and she opened her eyes.

A heartbeat later, she heard a bell ring as faintly as fairy laughter. Her eyes went wide. She knew it was the small bell on Tildy's collar. She lowered her hood and listened, straining to hear the bell again. Seconds later she heard something. It didn't sound like a bell, however. She was almost certain it was a muffled bleat. Beetle couldn't tell if the sound came from somewhere to her right or from straight ahead. Taking her best guess, she continued onward. Every ten paces or so, she called Tildy's name and paused to listen. At first, nothing. Time seemed to stretch out as Beetle slogged through snow nearly up to her knees. She peered around uncertainly, hearing only wind and her pulse whooshing in her ears.

Then she heard another bleat.

She swept the area with her flashlight. A dark mass flickered in and out of the white confusion. She scuffed closer. Her flashlight revealed the blurred mass of a dilapidated stone building. She saw an opening where a door had once been. Had Tildy taken refuge there? After wading through a snowdrift, Beetle cautiously entered the building.

The flashlight exposed a windowless room about the size of a one-car garage. Snow blew in through a large hole in the ceiling.

Broken roof rafters lay on the ground, scattered like giant Pick-Up Sticks. Tildy stood in a corner.

Beetle was flooded with relief. As she hurried toward the doe, her shins hit something. The next thing she knew, she was sprawled on her stomach. Searing pain gripped her as she rolled over and slowly sat up. She parted the ragged tear in both her jeans leg and pajama bottom and winced at the bloody scrape on her knee.

Keeping an eye on Tildy, Beetle scooped up a handful of snow and pressed it against the cut. As she waited for the snow to numb her pain, she realized she was sitting on a raised platform. She brushed some snow from its surface. A hint of rot reached her nostrils just as the boards beneath her started to buckle. Gasping, she tensed her legs and leaped off the structure seconds before the boards broke apart.

Beetle heard a huge splash. Spinning around on trembling legs, she shined her light through the jagged hole. Chunks of wood bobbed in black water below. Dank-smelling air rose from a stone-lined well. Trembling, she stumbled back and clasped her hand to her chest. What if she had fallen into the old well? She would surely have drowned.

She pulled herself together and limped to Tildy. Gently tugging on the doe's collar, she said, "Let's go, Tildy."

Tildy resisted and dug her hooves into the floor. Again, Beetle urged the doe to move. But the goat refused to budge. Then something crashed onto the roof. Beetle covered her head with her arms and leaned over Tildy as half the roof came down. When the cloud of snow and falling debris finally settled, Beetle could see a mass of pine boughs and broken timbers.

Apparently motivated by the noise and destruction, Tildy no longer needed persuading. The smell of pine sap in the room was dizzying. Beetle held on to the doe's collar as they worked their way around tangled tree branches and shattered timbers.

Wind snatched Beetle's breath as she stepped outside the building with Tildy. She pulled up her sodden hood and shivered as a lump of snow slithered down the back of her neck. The whiteout made it impossible for her to figure out where she was. How was she going to find her way back to the big barn?

Tildy suddenly took off at a run.

"Stop, Tildy," Beetle shouted, strengthening her hold on the doe's collar.

Tildy nevertheless bounded on.

Beetle reached out with her other hand and, without dropping the flashlight, managed a two-hand hold on the doe's collar. Unable to remain upright any longer, she dropped into a crouch and braced her body against the goat's flank. The scrape on her stiffening knee burned, and her sore shoulder throbbed. It took all of her strength to maintain the cramped position. If she let up for even a second, her feet would go out from under her.

Tildy's mad dash kicked up plumes of snow. Beetle winced and closed her eyes against the icy spray. Amid the confusion, it occurred to her that Tildy was heading down the slope. She doubted the doe could see where she was going in the swirling snow. The disturbing thought made her shudder as she imagined them colliding with an unseen obstacle.

All at once, Beetle's feet bumped over an uneven surface. She thought they might be crossing the footbridge above the ditch. Moments later, they skidded to a halt. She could hear the wind-lashed whirligig spinning nearby.

Breathless and aching from the wild ride, she let go of Tildy's collar and flopped onto the snow. After catching her breath, she shined the flashlight around. They were in front of the goat barn just beyond the fenced yard.

Beetle entered the goat barn with Tildy. The doe immediately ran down the center aisle and into the pen she usually shared with the other does. Beetle had lost sensation in her fingers and toes again. Snow coated her jeans, and her soaked sweatshirt hung from her shoulders like thick folds of elephant flesh.

The goat barn felt balmy compared to outside. The relative warmth made her want to curl up on the hay bales at the front of the barn. But Beetle had one more thing she wanted to do. The sky hadn't lightened yet. It gave her hope there was still time for her to return to the big barn and observe the game warden's reaction when he discovered the goats. She knew she was taking a risk. If the game warden caught her in or near the big barn, it was certain to make him suspicious. Still, Beetle couldn't resist seeing if her plan worked the way she hoped.

Tildy appeared content to stay in the doe pen, so Beetle left her there and closed her inside. Then she hastened out into the storm and closed the goat barn door and fence gate behind her.

Beetle limped across the footbridge. She followed the broad trail she and Tildy had plowed in the snow when the doe had rampaged down the slope. Before long, the trail veered toward the stone well house. Avoiding the turn, she continued uphill. She reckoned she would eventually reach the big barn.

The wind at her back aided her ascent. She switched off her light as the inn came into view. The yellow glow from the kitchen windows contrasted with the dark bulk of the barn. There were no signs of human activity.

Beetle took an indirect route to the big barn so no one would see her tracks. Arriving at its farthest corner, she followed a bare strip of ground that ran along the side of the building. She paused beside the barn door. Snow covered the goats' tracks, and there was no indication that anyone had entered the barn recently. There were only two possibilities: either the game warden had come and gone earlier, or he hadn't made his inspection yet.

Startled by the sound of voices, Beetle drew in a sharp breath. She slid the barn door open with trembling hands and bounded inside so she would not leave telltale footprints in the snow.

Beetle had barely closed the barn door before a man on the outside said, "Let's have a look inside."

Goose bumps prickled Beetle's arms. She recognized the game warden's voice. Heart pounding, she turned on her flashlight and hurried past the flock of goats in search of a hiding place. Midway in the barn, her light revealed some hay bales, layered like a wedding cake, about eight feet high and ten feet wide. Spotting a gap in the bottom tier, she dove inside and switched off the light. Billy got down on his knees and tried to crawl inside the cramped cavity with her. She pushed him away from the opening and prayed he wouldn't try again.

The barn door slid open before Beetle had time to catch her breath. She peered through a crack between the bales. A line of dark figures filled the doorway. Someone stepped forward and swept the room with a bright cone of light. Murtha's towering outline was easy to recognize. Beetle was wondering what was going through her mind when the woman suddenly buckled at the knees. Popshot and Deadeye broke her fall, then eased her, kneeling, to the floor. Did Murtha just have a heart attack because she felt powerless to prevent the game warden from discovering the deer? Panic-stricken, she fought the impulse to run to Murtha's side. Slugger unfastened the top buttons of Murtha's coat while Melvin Dooley slapped the back of her hand.

An overhead light came on, illuminating the barn's dark interior. Apparently unaware of Murtha's collapse, the game warden advanced with a confident gait. Beetle shifted uneasily. McNab had impressed her as the observant type. It bothered her that she hadn't had time to attend to details, like cleaning up the deer droppings. All she could do now was hope that deer and goat droppings looked enough alike to avoid his detection. She clenched her teeth and waited.

The hay bales started to shake. Beetle braced herself, wondering what was going on. It took a moment for her to realize that the goats were climbing on the bales. She frowned, annoyed that they had chosen the worst possible time to play King of the Hill. Then the entire structure shifted violently. Something hit the floor with a loud *whomp*. Beetle guessed it was a bale of hay. If the goats kept up their antics, they were bound to draw the game warden's attention to her.

Beetle stole a glance at Murtha. The woman still hadn't stirred despite the hunters' frantic efforts to revive her. To make matters worse, the game warden approached the spot where Beetle was hiding. Her heart felt like a lump of cold metal when he stopped in front of her hiding place. He was so close that Beetle could see the stitching on his shiny black boots. Hay dust tickled her nose. She pinched her nostrils together, barely thwarting a sneeze.

"Murtha, when did you move the goats to this barn?" McNab said, over his shoulder.

Without waiting for her answer, McNab strode to the opening in the partition and entered the next room. Billy scampered after him.

Beetle swallowed hard. Had she remembered to close the curtain? Did the game warden know about the tunnel? Craning her neck, she watched McNab approach the window she had left open a couple of days before.

"Flush claims he saw the deer in this window," McNab said, leaning in for a closer look. "There are smudged fingerprints on the glass. This window was opened recently."

Billy barged in beside the game warden. He stood up on his hind legs and plunked his front hooves on the windowsill. The crazy goat had probably acted on a whim, Beetle thought. Even so, she could have kissed him right then.

McNab paused. Beetle could barely stand the suspense. Then, he laughed. Stroking the buck's back, he said, "Billy boy, I think I know what happened here. Flush saw you or one of your friends in the window and thought it was a deer."

Billy twitched his short tail and baaed.

Beetle's hard work had paid off. But as far as she was concerned, Billy deserved most of the credit. Without him, her plan might not have succeeded.

McNab walked back through the opening in the partition. The thin smile on his face turned to shock when he saw the hunters scrambling to bring Murtha around. He immediately shouted an order to Melvin Dooley. "Get the deer carrier out of the back of my truck." Then to George Dooley, "There's a first aid kit in the glove compartment."

A few minutes later, the men returned with the requested items. "Let's get Murtha back to the inn," McNab said.

Deadeye and Slugger shifted Murtha onto the too-short canvas stretcher. Her legs hung beyond the foot end. Popshot and Floyd Dooley stepped up to lend them a hand. Each of the four hunters grasped a stretcher handle. Straining, they lifted Murtha off the ground and carried her out into the storm.

After all the hunters had cleared the barn, the game warden turned off the overhead light and rammed the door shut.

Billy at the window

Blueberry Wine

Beetle was anxious to find out how Murtha was doing. She counted to one hundred to give the men a head start. Then she crawled out of her hiding place, winced from the cut on her knee, and stood. She switched on the flashlight and began to make her way back to the cellar before the goats lost interest in munching hay and decided to follow her.

She lingered inside the cellar closet for a moment to prepare for the challenge of sneaking back into the inn. When she stepped out, she felt her stomach drop as she shined the light around.

Where were the deer? Then she heard low grunts and breathed in an especially strong scent of apples. She hurried to the back of the cellar.

Splayfoot snorted as Beetle approached the apple bin and let down his guard as he recognized her. As the does chomped apples, the fawns nibbled bits and pieces of fruit that had fallen to the cellar floor. Beetle doubted the deer would leave enough apples for Murtha to bake another pie. What would Murtha say? Beetle figured that was the least of problems at the moment.

She turned and headed for the cellar stairs. On the landing at the top of the stairs, she joined Jezebel near the kitchen door. She stowed her flashlight in her sweatshirt pocket, carefully lifted the latch, opened the door a crack, and peeked in. She stifled a gasp at the sight of Murtha lying motionless on the stretcher on the kitchen floor. The hunters stood around her, talking in worried tones.

Beetle eased the door open several more inches. Jezebel pushed past her and streaked across the kitchen, unnoticed by the men. The distance from where Beetle stood to the bedroom was about thirty feet, but it looked as wide as the Grand Canyon to her worried eyes. She had to make her move now, or she would talk herself out of it. Barely breathing, she slowly edged around the door and closed it silently behind her.

Her heart pounded as she got down on her hands and her good knee. She kept her injured knee raised off the floor, relying on her foot to help propel her along. Taking a steadying breath, she began her lop-sided crawl. She paused frequently, succumbing to the protests of her throbbing shoulder.

Her slow pace and awkward movements made minutes seem like hours. A floorboard snapped just as she came up behind Melvin Dooley. Beetle went rigid.

There was nowhere for her to hide. The only thing she could do was huddle close to the floor and pray she wouldn't get caught.

If Melvin heard the sound, he didn't show it. Beetle seized the opportunity to move on. The floorboard snapped again when she lifted her knee. This time Melvin looked over his shoulder. Fearing discovery, she racked her brain to think of a way to explain her presence and soaked clothing.

Melvin gazed right over her head, shrugged, and turned back around.

Instead of relief, Beetle suddenly felt the strain of everything she'd been through since sneaking out of the inn earlier that morning. She suppressed the impulse to curl up in a fetal position. She told herself she'd come too far to give up. She gritted her teeth and resumed her awkward crawl. As she passed behind the men, she kept her eyes focused straight ahead, fearing she would lose her nerve if she looked in their direction.

Safe at last, she collapsed on the bedroom floor. After only a moment's rest, she dragged herself up and flicked on the flashlight.

Then she pulled off her drenched sneakers and struggled out of her wet sweatshirt and jeans. Despite her discomfort, she kept her wet pajamas on to save time and covered them with a bathrobe. She stared enviously at Jezebel, fast asleep on the bed pillow. Then she picked up a corner of the coverlet and scrubbed her wet hair with it.

Bits of hay fell out. She hurried to the dresser, grabbed her hair brush, and vigorously stroked her hair until she was certain no hay remained. Beetle reentered the kitchen, pretending she'd been awakened by the commotion outside her door. She dodged between two hunters and emerged next to Deadeye, who cradled Murtha's head. Crouching stiffly, she slumped to the floor next to him.

The game warden knelt to Murtha's right, an open first aid kit at his side. He passed smelling salts under her nose. Beetle thought it was taking too long for Murtha to wake up. With growing concern, she put her hand on Murtha's shoulder. The motion caught the game warden's eye. He seemed to size her up in a single glance. Then he returned his attention to Murtha. Beetle looked nervously at the gun holstered on his belt.

McNab made another pass with the smelling salts. This time Murtha's eyes snapped open as she came to with a gasp.

"What happened?" she asked, blinking up at the circle of concerned faces.

McNab patted the back of Murtha's hand. "You'll be fine," he said. "You fainted in the barn, is all."

"Fainted?" Murtha knotted her brow. "But what about the—"

"Inspection," McNab said.

Murtha nodded.

"It's over. No deer. Just goats," he reported.

Murtha's eyes went wide and her lips parted. After a moment, she said, "Oh. Right. I didn't think to mention the goats earlier."

Beetle was relieved that Murtha had the presence of mind to hide her surprise.

"I reckon Manuel Flush mistook one of the goats for a deer," said McNab.

Murtha nodded slowly. "That makes sense."

"Lay still for a couple of minutes," McNab advised. He put two fingers on the inside of Murtha's wrist and stared at his watch for a short time. Looking up, he said, "Your pulse is normal. But you look pale. A glass of your blueberry wine should cure that."

Murtha pushed herself up onto her elbows. "Good idea."

"Tell me where you keep it, and I'll get a bottle," McNab offered.

"Down the cellar stairs on a shelf to the right. You'll need your flashlight," she added.

A wave of panic washed through Beetle as the game warden started across the kitchen. She instantly thought of the unlabeled bottles she had seen on the shelf. Her mind raced ahead, envisioning the calamity sure to follow when the game warden descended the stairs.

When Murtha attempted to stand on her own, Slugger and Deadeye helped her to her feet and guided her to a chair. Beetle sprang to Murtha's side. She had to tell Murtha that the deer were in the cellar before it was too late. While the hunters' backs were turned and their attention fixed on the game warden, she seized the chance to sneak her information to Murtha.

Just then, Jezebel burst out of the bedroom, caught up with the game warden, and cut in front of him. Weaving back and forth in his path, she slowed his approach to the cellar.

Beetle discreetly tapped Murtha on the shoulder.

Murtha twisted around and looked at Beetle, gave her a knowing look, then motioned for her to come closer. Beetle thought Murtha was going to whisper in her ear, but Murtha surprised her by sniffing at her instead. Then Beetle sniffed herself and detected Billy's stench on her hands.

"You moved the goats to the barn?" Murtha asked in a whisper.

Dry-mouthed, Beetle answered, "Yes."

Murtha scrunched her brows together and whispered, "Where are the deer now?"

Beetle pointed at the floor.

Murtha blinked, then looked around to see if anyone was nearby. "The cellar," she whispered.

Beetle bobbed her head.

Murtha spun in her chair. The game warden had already opened the cellar door. *"Morris, wait,"* Murtha called out, *"I've changed my mind. I'd rather have coffee instead."*

After what seemed like the longest minute of Beetle's life, McNab stepped back into the kitchen and closed the cellar door. Beetle saw a hint of confusion on his face when he turned around and started back across the kitchen.

Murtha looked at McNab and shrugged. "Sorry. I had a sudden hankering for black coffee."

"No problem, Murtha," he said.

At last, Beetle exhaled the stale air she'd been holding and took a deep breath. The deer were safe from the game warden for now.

When no one was looking, Murtha gave Beetle a broad smile, expressing her deep appreciation. The acknowledgment warmed Beetle's heart.

McNab filled a mug with coffee for Murtha. He handed it to her and pulled up a chair to sit beside her. The gold shield on his coat flashed as he craned past Murtha and looked at Beetle. "I don't believe we've met," he said.

Beetle braced herself, trying to appear as if she had nothing to hide.

"This is Beetle," Murtha intervened. "Her parents are Margo and Sheldon Beane. They came to Hickory about twelve years ago on an assignment. Remember?"

A smile softened the hard planes of McNab's face. His eyes shifted in a way that suggested he was revisiting the event in his mind. "Sure. I remember. When the townspeople heard that two scientists were looking for a rare species of dung beetle under the cow pies in Farmer Fleece's pasture, they came out to see the goings on."

McNab shook his head. "It was a high-spirited crowd. They brought folding chairs and picnic lunches. Vendors showed up, too, selling everything from hot dogs and ice cream to balloons and American flags."

Beetle furrowed her brow. This was the first time she'd heard that her parents had come to Hickory, let alone on an assignment.

"I don't know how the Beanes did it," McNab said, "but they got the crowd to take a real interest in their work."

Beetle wasn't surprised that her parents had been able to engage the crowd. Their enthusiasm for their work was infectious.

"Spotted dung beetles were thought to be extinct in Maine until the Beanes found a viable population on Farmer Fleece's land. It was designated as a dung beetle sanctuary because of their discovery," McNab said.

Beetle was thinking about how the ancient Egyptians had revered the dung beetle, creating sacred amulets in their image as well as depicting them in their hieroglyphs to symbolize death and renewal, until she noticed McNab staring at her with an unreadable expression on his face. She tensed. Had her sudden appearance in the kitchen earlier made him question whether she'd been in her room the whole time he'd been eating breakfast? And if so, was he thinking she could have moved the deer and replaced them with the goats before he made his inspection? She tried not to fidget under his continued scrutiny.

Beetle winced as the game warden lowered his hand, certain he was reaching for the handcuffs on his belt. He scrubbed his palm on his pants leg instead, then stuck out his hand. "Nice to meet you, Beetle. You'll have to pardon the way I . . . uh . . . smell," he said apologetically. "I patted Murtha's goat in the barn. A buck's musk can be *quite* strong."

Beetle knew exactly what McNab meant. She was relieved that he thought he was the only one in the room who smelled like Billy. Smiling shyly, she put out her hand.

After a brief handshake, McNab turned his attention back to Murtha. He waited for her to swallow a mouthful of coffee, then asked, "How do you feel?"

"I'm fine," Murtha said.

"If you're sure, I should start my rounds."

"I'm sure," Murtha said firmly.

McNab picked up the stretcher and folded it into the crook of his right elbow and then retrieved his first aid kit, also tucking it under his right arm. As he said goodbye to the group, he pulled an orange knit cap from his pocket with his free hand.

A small red and blue mitten was balled up with it. "I found this mitten on the barn floor this morning. Does it belong to you, Beetle?"

The mitten must have fallen out of her sweatshirt pocket, she realized with a start. Beetle thought her heart was going to burst out of her chest. Was he going to ask her where she had been earlier that morning? Somehow, she managed to find her voice and admit the mitten was hers.

Disguising her limp, she walked over to the game warden and took the mitten from him. She expected it to be wet—evidence that she had been out in the storm. But it was *dry* instead. She was reminded of the strange inconsistencies she had experienced in the swamp. A chill snaked across her shoulders. She summoned the courage to meet McNab's eyes. There was not a hint of suspicion in them.

Snow spiked into the hall when McNab opened the kitchen door. Pulling his cap on, he said, "This is the worst nor'easter we've seen in years. I doubt there will be many hunters out today." Then, turning up his coat collar, he stepped out into the storm.

Closing Day

Murtha's appetite came roaring back. Making up for lost time, she ate ten pieces of toast slathered with butter and honey and an entire apple pie washed down with two quarts of black coffee. Her hunger finally satisfied, she stood up from the dining room table, slapped her broad palms together, and asked, "Are you ready to go hunting, boys?"

"You can count me in," Popshot said, hooking his thumbs behind his plaid suspenders.

"Me, too," Slugger agreed. He raised his head and sniffed the air. Looking thoughtful, he stroked his bushy, gray mustache and said, "I've got a nose for Splayfoot, and I *swear* I caught a whiff of him just now."

Beetle stole a glance at Murtha to gauge her reaction to Slugger's comment. It was hard to know what Murtha was thinking behind her calm exterior.

Beetle's mind raced. It seemed doubtful that Slugger had detected Splayfoot's subtle, woodsy scent all the way from the cellar. Still, she had to take his claim seriously. She shifted anxiously in her seat, wondering if he was going to rise from his chair and follow his nose to the cellar door.

The hunters broke into gales of laughter.

Reddening, Slugger held up his hands and said, "Okay. Maybe I got a bit carried away."

The tense moment over, Beetle relaxed.

"We still have to finish the vote," Murtha said.

"We're ready to go," George said, answering for the trio.

Deadeye looked out a dining room window. He seemed to have second thoughts about going out in the storm. After a minute, however, he said, "I'm in."

"Good. That's everyone, then," Murtha said. "There are snowshoes in the second floor attic for anyone who wants a pair."

All the hunters agreed it was a good idea.

"I can take them up to the attic," Deadeye volunteered.

Murtha nodded. "Would you get my snowshoes, too?"

"Sure," Deadeye said. He motioned to the men, leading them through the hall and up the stairs.

Murtha crossed her arms over her chest and looked down at Beetle. "You left the window open in the barn."

Beetle nodded guiltily. "I'm sorry. The window was open for three days before I discovered it. But it was too late by then, apparently," she said miserably. "I was worried the game warden would arrest you and set the deer free. So I hurried out of bed to make up for my mistake."

Murtha didn't speak right away. Beetle's insides twisted. The longer the silence lasted, the more she expected a furious response. Murtha finally said, "You can't change what's happened in the past. The important thing is that you had the gumption to put things right."

Narrowing her eyes, Murtha asked, "How did you find out about the deer?"

Beetle fidgeted with the belt to her bathrobe. Murtha had gone easy on her so far, considering she had broken her promise to stay out of the barn. But that didn't mean she was out of trouble yet.

"Go on," Murtha said.

Beetle's throat felt as dry as a chalk tray. "It started when Jezebel opened the cellar door. The latch held when I tugged on the handle. I must not have checked it properly," she said remorsefully." I chased her down the stairs and into a closet, where I fell through the back wall and landed in the tunnel. I was about to go back into the closet because I thought Jezebel could be hiding in the ceiling. Then I heard her cry once and then again from somewhere ahead. So I followed the tunnel and ended up in the barn with the deer."

"It's not your fault. I should have closed Jezebel in her room. Then you wouldn't have felt obliged to chase after her," Murtha said.

Jezebel made a scrabbling sound as she crawled out from under the table and darted out of the dining room. Murtha followed the cat's departure with a scowl. When she shifted her attention back to Beetle, her face appeared careworn. "Can I depend on you not to tell anyone about the deer?"

"Yes," Beetle said, disappointed that Murtha felt it was necessary to ask for her silence. Hadn't she already proven her loyalty to both Murtha and the deer? Then again, Murtha hadn't been cross with her for failing to keep Jezebel out of the cellar, violating her promise to stay out of the barn, and leaving the barn window open, possibly the worst offense of all. Would Murtha be as lenient with her for entering the barn a second time? She braced herself, expecting Murtha to bring it up at any moment.

Murtha didn't mention Beetle's second foray into the barn. She patted her on the shoulder instead and said. "Moving the deer and replacing them with the goats was a brilliant plan. Did you have any problems getting both herds to cooperate with you?"

"No," Beetle said, without going into further detail.

"You were brave to go out in the storm," Murtha said. "If you had lost your way, you could have frozen to death. I think your parents would be lucky to have you come along on one of their missions."

"Thanks," Beetle said, smiling modestly. Yet she did not feel especially brave, considering all the blunders she'd made while carrying out her plan. Still, Murtha's words of admiration emboldened her to ask the woman if she was protecting the deer in the barn from hunters.

"If I answer your question, it will jeopardize their safety," Murtha said tightly.

Beetle was surprised and hurt by Murtha's clipped response. One moment Murtha was praising her, and the next she was cold and secretive. Her refusal neither to confirm nor deny Beetle's query suggested the deer could be facing a threat greater than hunters. Chilled by the notion, she tried to imagine who or what it could be.

Muffled thumps and bangs sounded from the attic above.

Murtha gazed up at the ceiling, then looked at Beetle, "I'm taking the men hunting to keep them away from the inn, so there will be less chance of them discovering the deer." Frowning, she added, "Both the deer and the goats need hay and water. But they can keep until I get back."

Beetle wanted to take care of the animals. But after Murtha's cryptic response to her question, she felt awkward around the woman. In a rush, she said, "Let me do it."

Murtha shook her head. "Thanks for offering, but you've done enough already. You should get some rest instead."

"No. I really want to do it," Beetle said.

"All right," Murtha relented. "That would be a big help."

"The deer might not be hungry," Beetle said.

"Why not?" Murtha asked.

"I found them eating apples out of the bin just before I sneaked back into the inn. "I'm afraid there won't be any left when they're done," Beetle answered in a small voice.

Murtha waved her hand and laughed. "I have plenty of blueberries preserved to bake with. As for the deer, you'd be surprised how much they can eat. Give them a bale of hay and two buckets of water. That will keep them until the hunters leave. The goats will need a bale, too, and just one bucket of water." You'll find everything you need in the big barn."

Despite Murtha's inscrutable personality, Beetle had grown fond of the woman. With a surge of emotion, she said, "I'm so glad you're all right. When you collapsed in the barn, I thought you had a heart attack or something."

"You were there?" Murtha asked as a frown creased her forehead.

Beetle nodded.

"I'm sorry you were frightened," Murtha told her. "I just got a bit dizzy. With all the excitement, I probably forgot to breathe. Besides, I'm as strong as a burl on an oak tree. Oh, before I forget to mention it, watch out for Claudine, the porcupine. She makes frequent trips to the tunnel from her den under the barn."

Beetle shuddered. "I met her already. She chased me out of the tunnel and into the barn. But she didn't get me with her quills."

"Thank goodness for that. Porcupine quills are very painful when they're embedded in your flesh. Having them removed is even worse."

"Is there some way to protect myself if I meet Claudine again?" Beetle asked uneasily.

"She won't bother you if you give her a few table scraps."

Beetle made a mental note to bring food for the porcupine on her next trip through the tunnel.

Footsteps thundered on the stairs. Moments later, the hunters filed into the kitchen with snowshoes in hand. The foot gear looked like wooden tennis rackets with leather netting and bindings. Deadeye handed Murtha an enormous pair that made the men's snowshoes look child-size.

Murtha gave Beetle a conspiratorial pat on the shoulder and then walked into the hall opposite the kitchen door. She emerged bundled in her plaid mackinaw, orange cap, and vest. Tucking her snowshoes under one arm, she flagged Beetle's attention. "I expect we'll be away for several hours. I'm sure you can find plenty to do while we're gone." Then, towering above the men, she turned and led them outside.

Beetle waited until the VW bus was out of sight, then hurried to her room and dressed in warm clothes. The numerals on the digital alarm clock glowed 10:00 AM. When she returned to the kitchen, it seemed eerily quiet. She looked out the window at the driving snow and shivered as though she were out in the storm again.

She retrieved her parka and boots from the hall and put them on. Her stomach rumbled, reminding her that she hadn't eaten. She took a corn muffin left over from the breakfast Murtha had prepared for the hunters and ate half of it. Saving the rest for Claudine, she slipped it into her coat pocket.

Flashlight again in hand, she went down the cellar stairs. Her light illuminated Splayfoot standing near the bottom step. Beetle guessed he was there to greet her. She looked into his eyes. "Everything is fine," she said. "The game warden searched the barn, and he's gone away."

Splayfoot tilted his antlered head and twitched his large ears.

"Murtha is out with the hunters and won't be back for a while."

The buck nodded and pawed the ground as if to say, You've done well. The does and fawns stood in a knot beside the old furnace. Beetle thought they might be bored, hungry, or both.

"I'll have hay and water for you soon," she assured them.

Beetle entered the closet and went through the secret door. She walked slowly through the tunnel and up the ramp. There was no sign of Claudine.

A snowy half-light seeped through the barn windows, but there wasn't enough light to see clearly.

Beetle turned on the overhead light and gasped. Hay bales had been knocked down and torn apart. Bedded down amongst the scattered debris, the culprits chewed their cud peacefully. Beetle heaved a sigh. She thought about cleaning up the mess, but it seemed like a waste of time while the goats were still in the barn.

Turning off and pocketing her flashlight, she heard a noise that sounded like someone sucking a thick milk shake through a narrow straw. She looked up in the direction of the sound and spotted Claudine snoring on a beam high overhead. Beetle thought the porcupine was almost cute with her arsenal of quills flattened down.

She collected three empty buckets scattered about the ruined bales and carried them to a spigot. As she filled one for the goats, something nudged her side. She turned just as Billy shoved his muzzle into her coat pocket and snuffled Claudine's half of the corn muffin.

Beetle felt she owed Billy for the stellar performance he'd put on for the game warden. Given that Claudine was not an immediate threat, she let him take the porcupine's share. She watched him run away with his prize and prayed it would keep him busy until she completed her task in the barn.

Placing the bucket on the edge of the trashed bales, she wasn't optimistic it would remain upright for long. She turned her attention elsewhere, walked toward the shadowy recesses of the barn, and flicked on her flashlight to see if she could find something she could use to haul hay to the deer. She panned the light across an assortment of hand tools mounted on the back wall. Farther on, she saw an old workbench with leather reins and a horse collar heaped together on top. Then she noticed a wooden toboggan stored beneath it.

Beetle pushed aside a veil of cobwebs, ducked under the workbench, and claimed the toboggan. She dragged it into the light by its rope, turned off the flashlight, and set it on the floor. By coincidence, the sled was a perfect size for Beetle and a passenger or two. After dusting it off with a handful of hay, she spotted the letters M B etched into the wood. Had the sled belonged to Murtha when she was a child? If so, was it possible that she and Murtha had once been about the same height? Beetle frowned, unable to picture Murtha ever being small.

Beetle found a bale of hay still intact and strained to roll it onto the sled. Then she inserted one of the remaining empty buckets inside the other and wedged them between the bale and the sled's curved bow. She glanced up, relieved that Claudine was still asleep. Then she turned off the overhead light, flicked on the flashlight, and left the barn through the tunnel.

After maneuvering the toboggan through the closet and into the inn's cellar, Beetle announced, giggling, "The hay wagon's here."

The deer raised their heads. Twenty-three pairs of eyes reflected the flashlight's beam as she parked the sled and closed the closet door behind her.

Beetle carried both buckets upstairs to the kitchen. She wondered if the bale of hay would still be intact when she returned. She filled one of the buckets halfway in the sink. Holding the flashlight in one hand and the heavy bucket in the other, she slowly descended the treacherous stairs as water sloshed on her jeans. She set the bucket down on the cellar floor, then returned to the kitchen and repeated the process.

Winded after setting the second bucket of water on the floor, she tucked the flashlight in the crook of her arm. The bale remained untouched. It seemed deer had better manners than goats. She rolled it off the sled. Two hemp strings bound the hay bale. The sharp stems of dried grass bit her fingers as she removed one string and then the other. The bale burst apart into a series of compressed biscuit-like sections.

The honey scent of mown grass filled her nostrils as she shook out each square section and spread loose hay over the floor. She closed her eyes and imagined she was standing in a summer meadow, the sun warming her face.

Suddenly, Beetle felt a wet tongue on the back of her hand. Opening her eyes, she looked behind her and grinned. It was a fawn. Now that he had her attention, he seemed content to scamper away. Beetle's amusement quickly turned to concern as it occurred to her that Murtha and the hunters might return early. She didn't want the hunters to see her leave the cellar and give them a reason to wonder what she had been doing down there.

She reluctantly started for the stairs. She climbed half way and paused with a sigh.

Would this be the last time she saw the deer? Taking a long, possibly last look, she shined the light on the spunky fawns, gentle grazing does, and Splayfoot, valiant defender of his herd. Then she reluctantly climbed to the landing and entered the kitchen.

The Last Entry

Beetle washed her hands, made herself presentable, then sat down at the kitchen table with her journal. It was still snowing hard. Light filtered through snow-wreathed windows and created a gloomy atmosphere in the room. The tin chandelier above the table cast a comforting glow on the blank page in front of her. Picking up her pen, she wrote:

Dec.6

Dear Journal,

I wish I didn't have to go home tomorrow. It seems like I just got here. Mom and Dad haven't called. I hope they're all right. I'd love for them to be home when I get back to Boston.

Beetle put down her pen. The thought of being stuck with only the Old Blister for company made her queasy. Her greatest wish was for Ms. Blister to marry and move far away. She thought Marley Swindell, the ghoulish undertaker, would make a perfect husband for the woman. Beetle hadn't seen a wedding band on his long, hairy ring finger. Smiling impishly, she pictured the newlyweds driving into the sunset with crepe paper streamers and chains of linked sausages tethered to the hearse's back bumper.

A fierce wind whistled through cracks around the windows and howled down the chimney. It sounded like a pack of hungry wolves.

Another gust rocked the inn on its foundation, trembled the walls, and battered the roof. How much punishment could the old house take, Beetle wondered.

Light from the chandelier dimmed several times, then went out. Beetle held her breath and waited. To her relief, the power came back on. But for how long?

Too jittery to concentrate on her entry, she quickly signed off. She got up and hugged herself for comfort. For some reason, she felt safer moving around.

She wandered toward the dining room. Glimpsing the bar, she remembered the paper Murtha had stashed inside it. More than likely, this would be Beetle's only chance to find out what the paper contained.

If it was a bill or letter demanding payment for overdue taxes, Beetle was certain her parents would be glad to help Murtha. But she had to find out what was on the paper first.

She approached the bar, knelt down, and gently tapped the raised panels with her knuckles. One of them yielded and slid back, exposing the paper cylinder inside a narrow, musty compartment. She removed it carefully. The yellowed paper appeared much worn from handling and far too old to be a recent tax bill.

Beetle brought it to the dining room table. Her nerves felt taut. A sweat mustache formed on her upper lip as she gradually unfurled the fragile tube. The wind launched another assault on the inn. Loose shutters banged like a volley of gunfire. Beetle paused to steady her hands before continuing. She didn't want to tear the paper.

When the paper finally lay open in front of her, pinned to the table by her forearms, Jezebel sprinted into the room and pounced, landing neatly on the table beside Beetle.

"Jezebel, you startled me," Beetle frowned. Her irritation faded as it occurred to her that Jezebel may have been frightened by the storm and come to the dining room seeking reassurance. Then, feeling a flush of guilt, she wondered if Jezebel could have heard the rustle of the paper being unfurled and come to investigate.

Beetle half expected Jezebel to give her a reproachful look. But the cat showed no interest in Beetle's invasion of Murtha's privacy and began to groom herself. Beetle turned her attention back to the paper and the ornate script at the top of the page. She caught her breath, suddenly aware she was looking at the Last Will and Testament of Barnibus Bellwether, dated the Twenty-sixth day of August 1735.

She assumed the will would be filled with a lot of dull legal terminology, but she was determined to find the answer to what was troubling Murtha. Faded ink and the fancy script made it difficult to read. What's more, some words contained a letter that looked something like an *f* but it had no crossbar. It took a while for her to figure out that the strange letter was an elongated *s*. Bearing old-fashioned spelling in mind, she tackled the document.

It began with Barnibus Bellwether bequeathing his entire estate to his oldest son, Ulysses. A herd of deer, an albino buck among them, was included in his holdings. Her heartbeat sped up.

Had the inheritance of the deer finally come down to Murtha?

The wind keened outside the dining room windows, but Beetle barely noticed as she eagerly read on. In the next paragraph, she learned that the last childless member of the Bellwether family was responsible for finding a successor to inherit the estate.

Finally, Barnibus required all subsequent heirs to sign his will and swear to do everything in their power to keep the outside world from finding out about the deer. Beetle browsed the column of names. She recognized several from the portraits in the grand room. Murtha's name was at the bottom. Beetle gazed intently at the woman's signature: *Murtha was the last living member of the Bellwether family*. At last she had discovered Murtha's troubling secret. Beetle had a sudden, disturbing thought. If Murtha should fail to find an heir, there would be no one to look after the deer. She wished she could help Murtha. But what could she do?

Her thoughts were interrupted by voices and the sound of stomping feet outside the kitchen door. Beetle jumped up. The paper furled as soon as she released it. She slipped the cylinder into the compartment and closed the panel. Jezebel remained on the table as Beetle hurried into the kitchen and snatched her journal and pen off the table. She made it to her room just as the hunting party entered the kitchen.

Beetle watched the bedraggled group file into the kitchen. They looked as if they'd spent the morning digging out from under an avalanche. The game warden trailed in behind the others. Seeing him gave Beetle a start. This time, she hoped the game warden was making a social call. Perhaps they had met on the road and Murtha invited him back to the inn.

The hunters hung their coats in the hall, then draped their hats and gloves over a wooden rack beside the hearth in the dining room. Before going to their rooms, Murtha provided the men with old towels to wipe down their guns.

Morris McNab volunteered to light the kindling and logs stacked in the dining room fireplace. Meanwhile, Murtha rinsed out the coffee urn and refilled it with water. She carried it to the counter where Beetle set out clean coffee mugs for the men. Keeping her voice low as she scooped fresh ground coffee into the urn's metal basket, Murtha asked Beetle if everything had gone all right with the deer and the goats.

Beetle nodded.

Murtha gave her a quick smile. "Good." She then pressed the urn's ON switch. The indicator light glared red.

Fifteen minutes later, outfitted in dry clothes, the hunters trooped back into the kitchen. They filled their mugs with coffee and carried them into the dining room. The hunters were sitting around the table when Murtha entered with an oversized apple pie in each hand. Beetle followed close behind with a stack of dessert dishes and a bundle of forks balanced on top. There was no sign of Jezebel. Beetle wondered where she had gone.

"Morris, do you think the men will be able to make it home tonight?" Murtha asked, cutting one of the pies into generous sections.

Morris looked up from prodding the blazing logs with a poker. "The storm is winding down. I expect the main roads will be passable soon."

"Didn't see any sign of Splayfoot," Slugger commented glumly as he passed a piece of pie to the hunter beside him.

Morris set down the poker and took a seat at the table. "The snow was coming down so thick, I doubt you could have seen him if he was standing right beside you."

"True." Slugger nodded."

"You are coming back next year, aren't you?" Deadeye asked Slugger.

"Of course. I can't wait to get another crack at Splayfoot," Slugger said.

"Glad to hear it," Deadeye said. "We've been hunting partners for years."

"I already made my reservation for next year," Popshot chimed in.

The Dooley brothers exchanged glances, and then Floyd said, "We'll be back, too. Maybe we'll bag some deer next year."

Jovial conversation filled the room as the men shared hunting stories. Beetle ate her pie, comfortably seated in an overstuffed wing chair to the right of the hearth. Watching the flames twist and swell in the fireplace, she had the guilty pleasure of knowing Splayfoot had spent the morning in the cellar of the inn.

The hats and gloves on the drying rack steamed gently as they emitted the smell of wet wool and mothballs.

Beetle thought she heard a distant rumble that sounded like rocks bouncing off a tin roof. The sound grew steadily nearer. She rose from her chair and put her empty dish on the sideboard. Then she hurried across the room to a window with a view to the street, careful not to bump the marble bust resting on a pedestal close by. The sculpture was of a man wearing a tricorne hat. He had a short pigtail at the nape of his neck. His steely gaze and the fierce set of his jaw suggested he might have been an officer in the Revolutionary War. Another ancestor of Murtha's, perhaps?

A shocking pink bus with a yellow snowplow mounted on the front thundered into view. Beetle's gaze widened as it barged into Murtha's driveway. Kicking up a curtain of snow, it nearly smashed into the back of the game warden's truck before slewing to a stop. The illuminated sign above the bus's front windshield read DESTINATION HEAVEN. Thirty or so metal frames, partially buried in snow, projected from its roof. Just as Beetle doubted things could get any stranger, two outlandishly dressed men emerged from the bus and shuffled down the snowy steps.

Murtha turned in her chair and glanced out a side window. "It's the boys from the highway department," she announced, getting up and starting toward the kitchen door. Curious, Beetle followed her into the entry hall.

the boys from the highway department

Beetle hung back a little as Murtha opened the door. She had to remind herself it wasn't Halloween as she observed the odd couple. The shorter of the two men said, "Hope you don't mind us stoppin' by for a cuppa coffee. The Scattershot Café is closed on account of the weather." He had a meaty nose and ruddy complexion. He wore a leather aviator's helmet and moth-eaten raccoon coat stretched tightly around his broad middle.

"Of course not, Hot Top Mike," Murtha said.

Hot Top Mike tilted his head at the tall, thin man beside him. "You've met Chuff Culpepper, I believe."

Murtha nodded. "Hello, Chuff."

Chuff grinned around a toothpick jutting out of the corner of his mouth. "Hi." His pronounced Adam's apple bobbed up and down as he uttered the single syllable. Beetle felt her eyes grow round like campaign buttons. With a mixture of revulsion and morbid fascination, she viewed the stuffed bullfrog mounted on the crown of his deerstalker hat. She wished she had her journal and a pencil handy.

Murtha dropped her gaze to a rust-colored chicken nestled in between the lapels of Chuff's double-breasted overcoat. "I see you brought Hortense."

"Got to. The highway department leases the bus from Farmer Fleece. Hortey's part of the bargain."

"Glad you brought her along," Murtha said. "Come in and warm up. There's plenty of pie and hot coffee."

"That's real nice of you," Hot Top Mike said. He glanced back at the bus, "Can't stay long, though. The Old Girl's headlights quit 'bout a mile back, and we've got more plowin' to do before dark. Farmer Fleece bought her from the Self-Centered Unicyclist's Universalist Church a couple years back and hasn't done any upkeep on her since." Hot Top Mike explained, frowning with disapproval.

So, a church had owned the bus. The metal racks on the bus roof, the destination on the sign above the windshield, and, possibly, its shocking color made sense to Beetle now in a strange sort of way. She thought the church's name had a New Age ring to it. As she returned to the wingback chair by the hearth, she wondered if the parishioners rode unicycles together on Sundays instead of attending religious services.

Chuff and Hot Top entered the dining room with their mugs of coffee. Their faces brightened at the sight of the cheery gathering. Hot Top bellied up to the table. Murtha passed him a piece of pie, and he immediately dug into it with a lusty grunt of approval.

Chuff was just about to sit down when Hortense squirmed out of his coat. Beetle raised her eyebrows as the hen flew across the room, squawking and shedding a trail of feathers before coming to land on the marble bust's tricorne hat. The adults hardly looked up from the table, as if they were used to seeing chickens act up in the house. Things like this only happened in movies, Beetle thought.

Hortense on the tricorne hat

Hot Top Mike began telling a story about how he and Chuff had once rescued a cat frozen to a railroad track downtown by melting its icy bonds with a cup of hot coffee from the Scattershot Cafe. The bullfrog's glass eyes twinkled in the firelight as Chuff nodded his turnip-shaped head throughout the story. At the end, he said, "Scattershot's coffee is strong stuff. It removed rust from the railroad track—made it shine like new. I mentioned it to the mechanic at the highway department, and now he uses it to keep his tools in good shape."

Hot Top looked at his watch. "Chuff and me got to go." He reluctantly pushed himself away from the table.

Chuff guzzled the remainder of his coffee, took the soggy toothpick from his plate, and stuck it back in his mouth. He traipsed over to the bust and picked up Hortense. She put up a fight, flapping her wings and pecking at his hands. Barely subduing the hen, Chuff held her against his shoulder with one hand and extracted an egg from the tricorne hat with the other. After Chuff had secured it in his pocket, Hortense permitted him to envelop her in his coat, and then he and Hot Top Mike bade the group goodbye and trudged back to the bus.

Rattlesnake Bluff

The hunters' trucks receded into the dusky sunset. Murtha and Beetle stood on the step outside the inn to see off the game warden. Morris started his truck. Leaving the door ajar, he emerged with an ice scraper in his hand. As he brushed several inches of snow from the front windshield, he said to Murtha, "Sorry I had to search your barn. I'll clear your name first thing in the morning."

"Thanks, Morris."

A burst of static erupted on the radio inside the game warden's truck. It was a police dispatcher calling for an officer to intercept a white Ford pickup truck traveling east on Greenbriar Road with a bull chained to its front bumper.

Morris briefly paused to listen to the radio transmission before he walked to the back of the truck and began to clean off the rear window and license plate.

"Roger that. I'm about a mile from there," the responding officer said.

Moments later, he reported, "I have the pickup in view. It's Manuel Flush's truck. The bull is dragging it from one side of the road to the other as if it were a toy. Rattlesnake Bluff is just up the road. Better call for backup."

Murtha raised an eyebrow. Beetle returned the quizzical look. Then she stared down at the step thoughtfully. When she had wished that Manuel Flush would get his comeuppance for beating his pigs, she hadn't meant for him to come to bodily harm.

"Why would Flush have chained the bull to his truck?" Beetle asked Murtha.

"Flush must have had the bull penned in the back of his truck," Murtha said. "I suspect he skidded into a snow bank and then chained the bull to the truck's front bumper to pull it out. Bulls are volatile creatures and not easy to control."

A siren wailed over the radio. The same officer said, "A hook and ladder truck just pulled ahead of me." After a suspense-filled minute, the officer came back with, "It's overtaken Flush's truck by several car lengths now. Able Rice is crawling out on the ladder with a noose on the end of a pole. He seems to be having a hard time lining up the bull, and Rattlesnake Bluff is less than a mile up the road."

Beetle held her breath.

Then the officer said, "*Able did it.* He looped the rope around the bull's neck and steered it away from the edge of the bluff just in time. Hold on . . . I'm getting out of the car."

The game warden said, "It sounds like the situation is under control. I might as well stay a few more minutes so that you can hear the rest of the story."

"I switched to my remote radio," The officer said, resuming his commentary. "Flush doesn't look too bad except for the white stripe running down the center of his hair. The paramedics attribute it to his harrowing ride."

Sirens barked and squawked in the background as the officer added, "Flush is thanking his rescuers. Wait a minute . . . The animal control officer and a state trooper just handed him a fistful of tickets. Flush has changed his tune. He's calling his rescuers a bunch of meddlesome do-gooders."

Sky Trip

When the game warden departed, Murtha opened the bulkhead doors. Splayfoot and his family bounded out of the cellar. Jets of steam plumed from the buck's nostrils as he pranced and pawed the snow-covered side yard. The high-spirited does and fawns leaped and twisted in a joyful dance.

Beetle stood at the edge of the spectacle clapping her hands with delight. When the deer ended their frolic, they headed soundlessly toward the orchard to the left of the inn. She felt a pang of sadness as they meandered around the gnarled apple trees and then melted into the snow-laden alders bordering the pine forest.

Wistfully turning her gaze back to where the deer had frisked in the snow, she noticed that Splayfoot had dropped an antler on the ground. The discovery made her heart beat faster. It felt like Christmas, the Fourth of July, and her birthday all rolled into one. She hurried over and crouched beside it. The instant her hand closed around the antler's rough base, a tingling sensation zinged through her mitten. The feeling intensified as it raced up her arm.

She tried letting go of the antler as she sprang to her feet, but her hand seemed welded shut. She could see Murtha striding toward her, waving and shouting. Suddenly a shrill noise resembling feedback from a loudspeaker filled her skull. It was impossible for her to hear Murtha's words. Then a brilliant white light flashed behind her eyes. Shaken and confused, she didn't know whether to attribute the series of frightening sensations to the antler or a malfunction in her brain. Within seconds, her body began to vibrate violently, and her blood fizzed like carbonated water.

She felt frozen on the outside and boiling on the inside. Then as improbable as it seemed, her body shot upward like a rocket. Everything was a blur. Wind throttled her ears and filled her mouth and nose as she tried to scream. She ascended higher and higher, bewildered and afraid. The dimming light rapidly turned to night.

The afterimage from the explosion of light behind her eyes finally faded. She was stunned to find herself on the surface of a comet. Dwarfed by the immense chunk of glowing rock and ice, she gazed down at herself and let out a horrified wail. Her body had become a hollow shell sheathed in luminous fibers, though the antler in her hand still appeared solid. It was as if she were looking at a hologram of herself.

It occurred to her that she might be dead. Was she on her way to the afterlife? She felt like throwing up, but she no longer appeared to have a stomach. All at once, the comet left her behind. She spun like a Frisbee in its wake, catching glimpses of its twin tails receding into the distance.

Beyond fear and reason now, she accepted whatever her fate might be. As she drifted weightlessly in absolute silence past planets, countless stars, and towering skeins of gaseous spirals, her mind became extraordinarily peaceful. She hardly blinked as two identical white bucks appeared at opposite ends of the heavens. They approached each other at astonishing speed and then collided and merged into a single magnificent white deer.

Beetle did not know what to make of it.

She stopped drifting. A second or two later, she plummeted feet first through the void. Wind bound her arms to her sides like steel bands. The stars looked like streaks of light as she continued falling at an ever alarming rate. Finally, the beautiful blue sphere of Earth shone ahead like a distant beacon. It ballooned in size as she hurtled

drifting weightless

toward it. She reentered the earth's atmosphere. In her insubstantial state, she experienced no harm. She saw huge cloud systems, continents, and vast glinting oceans. Through no control of her own, her trajectory arched toward the dark side of the planet. The nearly full moon revealed mountaintops and winding rivers shining like quicksilver as she sped ever closer to the earth's surface.

Below, thousands of vibrant beads of light came into view. Some were stationary while others appeared to stream along unseen pathways.

The tiny coursing lights thinned and eventually dissipated. Then only a scattering of fixed lights remained, bordered by a vast tract of forest. Beetle spotted the treetops of three imposing evergreens and the roofs of a large house and barn, and she knew exactly where she was.

Still holding the antler, Beetle crossed her arms over her chest and rolled into a ball as the ground rushed up to meet her. She let out a scream, envisioning her body shattering on impact. Instead something slowed her decent and cushioned her landing.

Her mouth remained agape when she opened her eyes. Dazed, she looked down at her body and anxiously observed her arms, torso, and legs. A long minute passed before she was convinced that her body was solid and unharmed.

Grateful to feel firm ground beneath her feet again, she blinked up at the night sky. Had her celestial journey been real or imagined? Her head throbbed as she scoured the remote stars, hoping they would supply the answer. But they shone diamond-cold and unreadable. A sudden attack of dizziness made her knees go limp. Two strong hands caught her from behind. "Are you all right?" Murtha asked.

"I don't know," Beetle said shakily. "I picked up Splayfoot's antler, and something strange happened. I . . . think I went into space."

"You did," Murtha said. "You must have had quite a shock. Take some deep breaths."

Beetle followed Murtha's advice. She sucked in mouthfuls of air, and watched her exhalations turn into puffs of vapor. After several minutes, she managed to gather her wits.

"Feeling better?" Murtha asked.

Beetle looked over her shoulder at Murtha and nodded weakly. "What happened to me?" she asked.

"Can you stand on your own now?" Murtha asked.

Straightening, Beetle answered, "Yes."

Murtha stepped out from behind Beetle and stood by her side. "After you picked up Sylvanus's antler, you went on a Sky Trip."

Beetle's mind worked furiously, trying to process what Murtha said.

"This is all so confusing," Beetle said, shaking her head.

"First, I should explain that Splayfoot is the legendary Albino. His true name is Sylvanus," Murtha said.

Beetle pictured the two white bucks merging into a single deer in space, and the spectacle began to make sense.

"Sylvanus left his antler for you, because he believes as I do that you are the person who can best take care of his herd after I'm gone. As the last Bellwether, I am required to pass on the legacy to a trustworthy person outside my family."

Murtha's announcement left Beetle speechless. She knew Murtha was looking for an heir, but she had no idea she would be chosen. When she recovered from her surprise, she asked, "Why did you and Sylvanus choose me when it was my fault the game warden came to search the barn?"

"Because you chose to protect the deer despite the risk of getting caught by Morris McNab," Murtha said.

Beetle looked at the antler in her hand. "You were going to explain what happened when I picked up the antler," she said.

"The enchantment on the antler released your shadow self from your body before I could prepare you for the transformation."

"I thought I was dying," Beetle said.

"The separation was necessary, though extreme; otherwise, you couldn't have survived the hostile conditions in space. The Sky Trip is an initiation that all guardians must go through to open their minds to the magical realm."

"Magical realm." Beetle ran the words through her mind. To her amazement, she could accept Murtha's explanation without reservation. She shifted her feet in an effort to stimulate her numb toes. Her thoughts returned to Sylvanus. "The legend of the Albino is true, then?

"Yes," Murtha said.

"But you told the hunters it was a lot of donkey dust."

"Admitting the legend was true would attract too much attention to the area," Murtha said.

Finally, Beetle had the nerve to ask Murtha, once again, if she was protecting the deer from hunters.

"Yes, for a very important reason: Sylvanus and his family are medicine deer."

Murtha's response set Beetle's heart pounding. "Medicine deer?"

Murtha nodded. "Medicine deer are immortal. Their immune systems are resistant to diseases, and they rapidly adapt to extreme changes in climate. Sylvanus and the does produce only male offspring. They possess their parents' unique traits, but their life expectancy is the same as a normal deer's. When the young bucks are able to fend for themselves, their mission is to establish a herd of their own and pass on their unique genes."

Beetle could hardly contain her excitement. "I get it," she said. "Medicine deer keep the wild deer population healthy. But why do Sylvanus and the does need protection from hunters if they are immortal?"

"That's an excellent question. A normal deer wounded severely by a bullet or arrow would leave a blood trail behind, whereas a medicine deer with an identical wound would heal instantaneously. Experienced hunters would find the lack of blood puzzling. If the anomaly repeatedly happened in this vicinity, state biologists could take notice and launch an investigation, which could lead to the capture of one or more of the medicine deer while they roam in the summer and subject them to testing in labs."

"You promised me before in the kitchen that you wouldn't tell anyone about the deer. Now that you know about their unique abilities, I want you to reaffirm your pledge," Murtha said.

Beetle's stomach twisted at the thought of the deer being imprisoned in a lab and exposed to cruel procedures. She rarely kept secrets from her parents, but this time was different. She nodded solemnly and said, "I swear I won't say anything."

"Thank you," Murtha said, then added, "Sylvanus and I are not the only ones to have recognized your resourcefulness and courage. You have also won the admiration of the Untamed Magic."

Spruce branches swayed in the wind, sloughing off clumps of snow.

"Who or what is the Untamed Magic?" Beetle asked.

"The Untamed Magic is an ancient entity who informs and sustains the natural world," Murtha said.

Beetle's mind raced. Was the Untamed Magic an invisible force or a jinn-like presence surrounded by roiling smoke and lightening?

"Again, I have to stress the importance of total secrecy. If the Untamed Magic's existence became known along with my ability to communicate with it, reporters, the NSA, FBI, CIA, and Homeland Security would descend on the inn — not to mention religious organizations. Unscrupulous corporations, wanting to steal the Untamed Magic's secrets, would send their people as well. Your parents could even be drawn into the mess."

"You can depend on me," Beetle said, restating her allegiance.

"Are there other guardians?" she asked.

"Yes. There are many around the world. But, the Untamed Magic is the only one that knows who they are, where they live, and which species of medicine animal they protect."

Beetle considered Murtha's answer. She wondered if there were medicine insects. And if so, why were so many going extinct.

The wind kicked up snow, sending it swirling around Beetle's feet.

"As my successor, you must also protect the local environment from people who deliberately pollute the land and exploit its finite resources," Murtha continued.

An owl hooted in the darkness.

"I realize this is a lot to take in," Murtha said. "It might ease your mind to know the initiation is not binding without your consent. Think it over carefully before you decide, because the commitment is permanent."

"What will happen if I turn down the inheritance?"

"Your life will be the same as always. The only difference is you will have no recollection of your stay at the inn. Your parents' knowledge of me will be erased as well."

Beetle felt a sinking sensation in her stomach. "How old do I have to be to give my consent?"

"Twelve," Murtha said.

"I will be twelve in May," Beetle volunteered.

"Then I'll expect your answer in six months," Murtha said.

Beetle blinked, suddenly aware of the intricate patterns of individual snowflakes glittering like multicolored gems on the ground. Next, she heard the faint scrabbling of a mole tunneling beneath the snow.

"I'm hearing and seeing things that I never thought possible," Beetle said.

"The initiation has heightened your senses," Murtha said. "The enhancement will wear off soon, but it will give you an idea of the observational powers you will develop during your apprenticeship," Murtha said.

Beetle's heart and mind expanded with joy as she pondered the thrilling possibilities.

"If you choose to become my heir, your training will begin this summer," Murtha said.

Beetle took a deep breath. Reasoning that she needed time to determine whether she was capable of fulfilling all that would be required of her, she overcame the impulse to give her consent even though it would not count until she turned twelve. Sensing their conversation beginning to wane, Beetle queried Murtha with more questions. "Given the secrets you are keeping, why did you let me come to the inn?"

"I tried every excuse I could think of to dissuade your mom," Murtha said. "She had no idea what she might be getting you into by sending you to the inn. But she managed to overcome all of my objections, and I finally agreed. Is there anything else you would like to know?"

"Are the hunters your only guests?"

"Yes. Although I did make an exception for your parents, because I thought their work was important, and the medicine deer were summering in the forest at the time."

"What do you tell people that show up at the inn without reservations?" Beetle asked.

"The Untamed Magic has enchanted the inn to make it appear barely habitable to the outside world. That usually keeps callers from coming to my door. If that doesn't work, the Untamed Magic conjures up a dragon to send persistent types away with no lasting memory of their fright."

When Beetle had seen the ferocious monster on the inn's roof, she had assumed it was a hallucination, never suspecting she had witnessed magic. "I saw the dragon on the day I arrived," she said, frowning.

"The dragon has never confronted an approved guest before. Given the fact that it presented itself to you makes me think the Untamed Magic was testing your nerve right from the start," Murtha said.

"I was really scared," Beetle said.

"But you didn't run off like all the others," Murtha said in a complimentary tone.

Beetle raised her eyebrows, taking Murtha's comment to heart.

"What does the inn look like without the enchantment?" Beetle asked.

"Beautiful," Murtha chuckled. "If you become my heir, you'll be able to see it for yourself."

Beetle recalled the afternoon when the brilliant shaft of sunlight gilded a section of the inn and made it appear grand and inviting. She had attributed the fleeting transformation to a trick of the light. Now she wondered if the Untamed Magic had allowed her a glimpse of the inn in its original state.

"If outsiders are rarely allowed to come to the inn, how have you been able to conduct your search for an heir?" Beetle asked.

"I hired a number of young people in Hickory to do odd jobs here so that the Untamed Magic could assess their potential," Murtha said.

"Did the Untamed Magic take an interest in any of them?" Beetle asked.

"No. You are the first."

A lone coyote howled eerily from somewhere in the forest. Soon the surrounding area was alive with a chorus of coyote song.

Beetle could not help feeling pleased about being the only young person selected, but she did not let it go to her head. Instead, she turned her attention to a question she'd been wondering about. "Are you concerned that the hunters might discover the deer?"

"The advantages of having the hunters stay at the inn outweigh the risks. It allows me to promote ethical hunting practices, especially among inexperienced hunters like the Dooley brothers. What's more, most people would never think to look for deer at the home of a reputable hunting guide."

The warmth was rapidly draining from Beetle's body. She shivered uncontrollably in the frigid air. Tucking the antler under one arm, she pulled up the collar of her coat.

"You're cold," Murtha observed. "We should go inside."

Beetle nodded in agreement. She took a rumpled Kleenex from her coat pocket and wiped her nose with it.

Murtha and Beetle walked about ten feet, then paused in front of Jezebel's bedroom window. The cat perched on the windowsill, observed them through the glass. Her eyes glowed eerily, reflecting the moon-bright snow.

All at once, Beetle heard an impish voice say, *"I knew you'd be chosen as Murtha's heir. You just needed a push in the right direction."*

Beetle shot Murtha a quizzical look. "Did you just say something?"

Murtha shook her head. "No. Your initiation has temporarily enabled you to hear Jezebel's thoughts."

After everything Beetle had experienced, she hadn't anticipated this surprise. With a sudden rush of anxiety, she asked, "Can Jezebel hear what I'm thinking, too?"

"No. Jezebel can't read minds. But she can receive your thoughts telepathically if you open them up to her."

Beetle breathed a sigh of relief.

"Jezebel and I share thoughts with one another regularly," Murtha said. "She predicted you would become my heir moments after she chased you out of the cellar. Knowing Jezebel wouldn't be satisfied until her prediction came true, I made her promise to mind her own business."

Murtha paused, then said, "After you told me you liked to draw from nature, and I became aware of your fertile imagination, I realized that Jezebel could be right. You see," Murtha went on to explain, "Creative people tend to look at the natural world with a sense of wonder bordering on belief in magic."

Murtha's explanation rang true with Beetle. While drawing outdoors, she often thought there was more to nature than science could ever explain. "Although you showed potential, a test was also involved. The Untamed Magic set up a challenge to test your loyalty to me and the deer," Murtha said.

"Did you know about my test?" Beetle asked.

Murtha shook her head. "I have nothing to do with testing."

"So, the Untamed Magic picked me as a candidate and set a test? Then what happened?" Beetle asked.

"After you passed the test, The Untamed Magic, Sylvanus, and I made the final decision, together unanimously agreeing to make you my heir," Murtha said.

"Protecting the deer was my test," Beetle said.

"Yes," Murtha said.

Murtha turned her attention to Jezebel. She folded her arms over her chest and frowned as she spoke to the cat. "You broke your promise, Jezebel. You shouldn't have led Beetle to the deer."

It suddenly occurred to Beetle that, after leading her to the deer, Jezebel had intentionally distracted her from closing the barn window, setting off the chain of events that had led to her being tested by the Untamed Magic. Thus, the test must have begun when Jezebel had gotten past the latch on the cellar door. Since Beetle was temporarily granted the ability to communicate with Jezebel, she sent the cat a question: *Did the Untamed Magic lift the latch for you?*

Jezebel twitched her tail. Silence.

Beetle wondered if Jezebel heard her question or if she chose to ignore it.

Jezebel's eyes blazed. "*Yes.*"

"I shouldn't give Jezebel the case of sardines I had promised her on condition that she behaved," Murtha said more to herself than to Beetle. "But considering how things turned out, I'll give it to her anyway."

Jezebel's cheeks bunched into what looked like a smug smile.

Beetle wanted to be angry at the manipulative cat, but she could muster only mild irritation. Frowning, she said to Murtha, "You said my ability to hear Jezebel's thoughts is temporary. Will it be restored if I become your heir?"

"Yes," Murtha said.

"I'm not sure if that's a blessing or a curse," Beetle said.

"A little of both, I'd say." Murtha's mouth twitched into a wide smile.

Beetle grinned tentatively. Then she began to laugh.

Acknowledgments

I am grateful to my editor, Marcia Gagliardi, for her insightful guidance and support throughout the publishing of this book. Many thanks to Lisa Freitag for her technical assistance. Thanks also to my first readers, my long-time friend, Candace Curran, and her husband, Walt Owen.

And most of all, thanks to my husband, John Lindgren.

Elizabeth Lindgren

About the Author

Elizabeth Lindgren is a Sasquatch fan and a friend to fairies. For inspiration, she wears an Elmer Fudd cap and shares her writing space with a tin goat, cement toad, seven-foot wooden giraffe, and her bicycle. Apart from writing and drawing, she designs and sews whimsical fish, dragons, pixies, and seahorses. Her home is in central Massachusetts.